T M Alexander

Labradoodle

Loose

RED PAINT

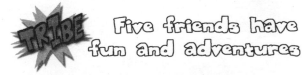

Five friends have
fun and adventures

PICCADILLY PRESS · LONDON

For Beth,
my lovely niece

First published in Great Britain in 2011
by Piccadilly Press Ltd,
5 Castle Road, London NW1 8PR
www.piccadillypress.co.uk

A catalogue record for this book is available from the British Library.

ISBN: 978 1 84812 133 1 (paperback)

1 3 5 7 9 10 8 6 4 2

Printed in the UK by CPI Bookmarque, Croydon, CR0 4TD
Cover design by Patrick Knowles
Cover illustration by Sue Hellard

Mixed Sources
Product group from well-managed
forests and other controlled sources
www.fsc.org Cert no. TT-COC-002227
© 1996 Forest Stewardship Council
FSC

Fifty's Kidnap

Biscuits For Breakfast

Fifty came round at half-past eight in the morning, which was odd because it was half-term and all normal eleven-year-olds were in bed. I got the door because Mum had left for work with Flo (who was going to her new best friend's house) and Amy was still asleep (and would be until lunchtime). I would have been asleep too but I forgot to draw my curtains so the sun lasered through my eyelids at six o'clock.

'What's up?' I asked.

He grunted. That was odd as well – Fifty likes to talk. I got the biscuit tin out – sugar's his favourite thing. He took a bourbon, ate it, took another.

'So what's up?' I said again.

He ate the second bourbon. 'Nothing.'

There was no point trying to fool my I've-known-you-since-you-wore-Thomas-the-Tank-pyjamas lie detector. I gave him a look.

He sighed. 'Probably Rose has gone to nursery.' His little sister is actually just 'Rose' but they didn't decide on her name for weeks so everyone went around saying 'She's probably Rose' and it stuck.

'So?' I knew Fifty didn't want his mum to send his little sister to nursery but I wasn't sure why. I went to nursery. So did he. Copper Pie's mum *runs* a nursery. So what?

'She went yesterday for the morning and she *didn't* like it.' He stuck his bottom lip out.

'How d'you know?'

'She told me, of course.'

Yeah, right! Rose can say 'yes', 'no', 'yoghurt' and 'star' (which means lightbulb). That was it. I decided to change the subject. Fifty is far too obsessed with his sister. 'Mum's left us some stuff for a Tribe picnic. She said there's loads, enough for two Tribes.'

Fifty grinned. 'There's only one Tribe.'

'We could take it to the park. Meet everyone there,' I said.

'Same,' said Fifty.

I looked at my watch. 'At . . . ten o'clock?'

'OK.' He got out his phone. 'I'll text the Tribers.'

I got crisps, Marmite, bread and the packet of chocolate

cakes out of the cupboard. And ham, cold sausages, pork pies and butter out of the fridge. While we made the sandwiches the texts came back: *yes* from Jonno, Bee and Copper Pie. The Tribe picnic was on. There were four days left of the holidays. It was sunny. *Ace.* I crammed the picnic and a rug in my rucksack.

'What about drinks?' said Fifty.

'We can buy them from the ice-cream van.'

We were off. It's not far to the park, but it seemed forever because Fifty stressed about his sister *all* the way. I adopted the usual strategy, which is to answer 'Yes' or 'Umm', or nod.

'You know they just leave the babies in those bouncy seats.'

'Yes.'

'And don't change their nappies.'

I nodded.

'Kids get bitten at nursery.'

'Umm.'

'You got bitten by Annabel Ellis *every* day.'

That needed a proper response. 'There *won't* be an Annabel Ellis at her nursery,' I said confidently.

'Let's hope not. Because if anyone upsets Probably Rose, they'll have *me* to deal with,' said Fifty. As he's small (half the size of everyone else –'Fifty' percent, get it?) and cute-looking, it didn't seem much of a threat. I would have completely forgotten about it, except that he said it again later, but not to me this time . . . to the police.

Needed –
One Dog

Bee was swinging on the gate to the play area, making it clang really loudly. 'Hi,' she said.

'Anyone else here?' I asked.

'Doodle,' she said.

'That wasn't what I meant.'

'You're anyone, aren't you, Doodle?' Bee stroked his head. She used to hate him because of the chewing (of shoes), dog hair (in her breakfast) and yelping (in the middle of the night). It was when Jonno went puppy training with her that it got better. Now they always carry dog treats in their pockets.

'Rose is at nursery today,' said Fifty. 'And not getting picked up till *two.*'

'Lucky Rose,' said Bee.

As she spoke I heard a familiar noise. We knew to move, and sharpish – it was Marco on his mountainboard accelerating our way. We all leapt onto the gate. *Clang!* He turned at the last second – just before certain impact – flipped his board in the air and caught it. Unreal!

'Hello, Marco,' said Bee.

'Hi. Can I lend the dog?' It was an odd thing to say. Marco comes from Portugal but his English has got pretty good since he's been at our school.

Bee used her favourite (and only) Portuguese word. '*Que?*'

'The dog.' Marco pointed.

'Why do you want Doodle?' said a voice. It was Jonno, glasses on the end of his nose as usual, with Copper Pie.

Marco tried to explain. We didn't understand. He gave up, got a stone and drew a picture on the pavement of what he wanted. It was a boy on a board with a dog dragging it along, like a husky.

'Why do you want to do that?' said Jonno, pushing his frizzy hair back.

'I see a boy, going fast with a dog.' It sounded fun. We all looked at Bee to see if Doodle was going to be allowed to be a husky.

She moved her black fringe out of her eyes. 'OK, but me first.'

We went over to the other side of the park by the big hill where there are always kids doing tricks on bikes and skateboards. Bee put her feet in the strappy bits on the board, bent forwards and stuck her bottom out. That wasn't going to work. Marco tried to straighten her up but the wheels moved and she yelped and grabbed on to him. Doodle sat at the end of the lead having a good gnaw on Copper Pie's black trainers. I didn't bother telling him.

'Try without the dog,' said Fifty.

Bee handed the lead to Jonno. 'What now?' she said.

'Move the knees,' said Marco.

She did. The board moved, but Marco steadied it. She fell off anyway. *Learning to mountainboard might take a while*, I thought.

Bee kicked the board over to Marco. 'You show me.'

When you can already do something without thinking it's really hard to show anyone else. I'm like that with surfing. Because I can do it without trying, I have to kind of watch myself do it in my head to explain it to anyone else. Marco didn't even try. He just scooted off, perfectly balanced, did a jump to turn and sailed back. That was the only lesson Bee was getting.

'It looks easy,' said Jonno.

'Can I go with the dog?' said Marco.

Bee nodded. Jonno handed him over. Marco waved the lead, which I think meant 'Go'. Doodle stayed by Copper Pie's tasty trainer. Marco did it again. Same result.

'I think you'll have to move first,' said Jonno. 'Doodle can't read your mind.'

Marco pushed off. Doodle got up and ran behind. That wasn't what Marco wanted. He came back over. 'How can I make the dog do the pull?'

'He needs something to chase,' said Fifty. 'Like a rabbit.'

'What about me?' said Bee.

Lots of nodding. Bee jogged off. Doodle watched her, but didn't follow. Bee stopped by the hedge.

'Doo-dle,' she shouted. He went off like a rocket. Marco shot forwards, lost the lead, fell backwards – splat. Doodle ran over to Bee and was rewarded with something from her pocket.

'Again,' said Marco. Bee rolled her eyes. It was never going to work.

'Once.' She held up one finger. 'Once more, that's all.'

He nodded and took back the lead. This time when Bee shouted for Doodle to come, Marco was ready. They went off at a good dog speed, following Bee. She ran in a big circle and stopped back by us, panting. Marco sailed round after her like he was the captain of a ship coming into port after a splendid victory. He patted his labradoodle-husky.

'Good dog,' he said. Bee fished about for more treats. Doodle gulped them down – I don't think dogs chew – and started barking.

'Shhhh,' said Bee.

Doodle nudged the board with his nose.

'He wants another go,' said Fifty.

'Me next,' said Copper Pie. He grabbed the lead. This

time Bee didn't have to run ahead. Doodle shot straight off, with only one of Copper Pie's feet strapped in. He managed to stay on, wobbling a bit. Doodle headed for the slope. Oh no! Disaster. Copper Pie obviously thought the same. He bailed out and the board accelerated away followed by Doodle. Copper Pie ran after him. He's a really fast runner but Doodle was faster. Luckily he decided to stop and chew a bone-like branch or Copper Pie would never have got him.

'My turn,' said Bee. 'I get it now.' She got on, bent her knees, said 'Run, Doodle,' and amazingly she stayed on. She even managed to steer him away from the hill and ride all round the grassy area. It was cool. Dog-power.

'It must be me next,' said Jonno. Bee handed over the lead. Doodle started dragging Jonno without the board.

'Sit,' said Jonno. Doodle jumped up at him. Jonno did the whole turning away thing that you're meant to do if a dog's naughty.

'You may as well have your go,' said Bee. 'Doodle's over-excited.'

Jonno didn't seem to like speed so he kept leaning back and yanking on the lead to slow Doodle down. They were like a remote control car being operated by a two-year-old. Stop. Start. Stop. Start.

'I give up,' said Jonno. He looked at me. I shook my head. I figured I'd be OK on the board, but I didn't fancy a manic dog dragging me along the ground, taking all the

skin off my knees. I think Fifty felt the same. So Marco had
a go. He went all the way down the hill on his board, mega
mega fast. The ball-bearing noise from the wheels was
super-loud. At the bottom, Doodle leapt up at Marco,
barking his head off and nearly knocking him over. It was
top entertainment, but eventually Copper Pie demanded
lunch, so we abandoned the very successful husky racing,
and Marco, for nosh.

Nosh

I laid out the rug.

'Who votes Keener be called Tribe Mother?' said Bee, tying Doodle up.

'Who votes Bee has no cake?' I said back. It wasn't witty but my brain doesn't make up clever things quickly, or in fact slowly.

'Only joking, Keener.' She smiled. I threw the bag of cold sausages at her. She shoved them away.

'Where are the chocolate cakes, Keener?' asked Fifty.

'Staying in the bag till we've eaten the rest,' I said.

'OK, Tribe Mother,' said Fifty.

I ignored him. Copper Pie was already scoffing sausages. He doesn't chew, just like Doodle.

'Pass the sausages.' I took two. Jonno picked up a roll,

peeled open the bun to look inside and dropped it like he'd been bitten. Marmite does that to people. Copper Pie picked it up and demolished it in two mouthfuls. Animal.

TRIBERS' FOOD FACTS

BEE: Likes organic, home-made stuff.

COPPER PIE: Likes unhealthy stuff – crisps, pies and sausage rolls.

JONNO: Eats grown-up food no one else has heard of.

KEENER: Hates runny food.

FIFTY: Gets fed brown rice cakes but wants golden syrup on everything.

I was thirsty, so I offered to get the drinks. Fifty came too. While I stood in the queue for the ice-cream van he swung on the play area gate, clanging it just like Bee had. He was probably watching all the toddlers fall off the end of the slide in the play area. They don't have brakes.

I heard the mountainboard wheels buzzing again and Marco zoomed past the queue. 'Thank you for dog.'

It's funny when he doesn't put all the words he needs in, or puts in too many. I watched him do a jump. It looked fun. I wondered why I'd never had a skateboard. Because no one had ever bought me one was the obvious answer.

I had to call Fifty *twice* to get him to come and help me with the cans. There was obviously something going on in the play area. Maybe there was a toddler having a lie-on-the-floor-and-kick tantrum or, even better, wrestling babies.

After we had a can each there was a burping contest, thanks to Bee who can never drink a fizzy drink without her stomach immediately expelling all the bubbles. There was a thought hovering in my head – *I can surf so I should be able to mountainboard*. It was followed by a second thought – *Dog-powered boarding would be cool*. And that one turned into action. I got up.

'Bee, can I borrow Doodle?'

'He's not a library book,' she said.

Lots of laughing, which I ignored. 'I'm going to have a go on Marco's board.'

'I suppose so,' she said, with a can-you-believe-Keener's-actually-going-near-my-dog face.

I untied the lead, which was attached to a bike rack, said 'See you,' and went in search of Marco.

Tricks

As we walked along, Doodle kept turning round and looking back at Bee. It was as though he knew I wasn't a proper dog handler. I tried not to catch his eye. I'm not exactly scared of dogs, I just don't like their teeth.

I could see Marco up ahead, trying out tricks on the path.

'Marco,' I shouted. He looked up and smiled. 'Can I have a go on your board with the dog?'

'Sure,' he said. 'You're a good surfer, makes good boarder.' Marco's been surfing with me. He's amazing.

'I hope so,' I said, but I wasn't sure. Surfing on water is a bit different from four wheels on bumpy ground. And falling in water, or a wipe-out as we surfers call it, is most definitely better than a tumble on the concrete.

He pushed the board with his foot, I stopped it with mine. So far so good. Marco waited for me to get on, but I didn't. It's embarrassing when you have a go at something you can't do, or don't know if you can do. I wanted him to go away, or at least turn round, but I couldn't say that to him, could I?

'You want help?' he said.

I nodded and handed over the lead. Marco hooked the loop over his foot. *Funny way to keep hold of a dog.*

'OK,' he said. Marco wasn't a bad teacher. Or maybe I was a good pupil. He showed me which foot to put at the front (your leading leg), how to get on without the board slipping away (make sure it's on the flat) and how to use your knees, heels and toes to move and steer. I messed about a bit at the top of the hill. It was easy.

'Down the hill,' said Marco.

I looked down. I've walked down the hill loads of times. I've run down it, cycled down it. But I've never gone down it on four wheels, without brakes.

'Go . . .' Marco couldn't find the word he wanted. He used his hands instead. They pointed diagonally. That made sense. I was going to slip my front foot out of the binding to turn the board to face the direction of Marco's hand but he shook his head and did a little jump. I got it. I was meant to jump to turn the board round. *Here goes*, I thought.

Jumping with a board attached to both your feet was

weird. But it worked. I was ready. I bent my knees, the board set off with me on it. I headed across the slope, and only remembered when I needed to turn and head the other way that Marco hadn't explained how to turn. *Great!* Or how to brake. *Even more great!* Luckily, it turned out to be just like surfing. I'm goofy (that means right foot forward – left foot forward is 'natural') so I just leant back on my heels and round I went. I did a few turns on the way down and to stop I turned back up the hill. Marco started clapping. I bowed. Time to try it with the dog!

But Where Is The Dog?

While I pushed the board back up the hill with my foot, I decided *I* was getting a mountainboard. My birthday's in November but there was a chance I could afford one before then if a lot of people forgot to pick up their pound coins from the swimming lockers. (I have lessons on Saturday mornings. I check the lockers, before and after. It's easy money.)

What is a mountainboard?

It's like a skateboard but it's bigger and the wheels aren't hidden underneath, they stick out the side. And there are bindings, like on a snowboard, to slip your feet in. That helps *you* do jumps.

> What is a mountainboarder?
>
> A lunatic that loves speed and danger.

'Great stuff,' said Marco.

'Wait till you see me with the dog,' I said.

'Dog,' he said, as though he'd never heard the word before. And certainly never used one as a husky. Or had the lead of one looped round his foot less than five minutes before.

'Dog,' I repeated.

A few very bad thoughts smacked me in the face, one after the other: *I'd left Doodle with Marco, Marco was standing in front of me, Doodle wasn't, Marco had lost Doodle, but I'd taken Doodle from Bee, so I was in charge, so I'd lost Doodle.*

Panic
Stations

I grabbed Marco by the shoulders. 'What have you done with Bee's dog?'

'Bee's dog,' he said. He smacked his forehead. It made a slap sound. Must have hurt. 'Bee's dog,' he said again. He looked down at his foot as though Doodle might still be attached to the lead that he'd looped round his trainer. Nope. Just a trainer, all on its own. He looked up at me, and made a big-eyed sad face. I looked all around, 360 degrees, ready to call out Doodle's name. But there was no point shouting. There were kids and bikes and prams and a bloke with a kite, but no dogs. And definitely no labradoodle.

'We've *got* to find Doodle,' I said. 'Or Bee will *kill* us.'

Marco nodded. 'I go,' he said.

'Go where?' I said.

'Round,' he said, waving his arm randomly at the grassy area. He pushed off and disappeared. Wheels buzzing.

I stood, deciding what to do.

WHAT MUM SAYS TO DO IF YOU'RE LOST

• Ask someone with children, preferably pushchair-size ones for help.
• Go back to the last place you saw who-ever you're meant to be with.
• Ask a policeman for help, if there's one handy.
• Stand still.

None of the tips from Mum helped with Doodle. I tried my own.

Go back to the picnic by the play area, in case Doodle has run over to Bee (but that would mean confessing if Doodle wasn't there). Run around the park, the roads nearby, everywhere, shouting loudly. Get a search party together of all the people in the park (except Bee). Hide, and hope Doodle reappears. Buy a steak and flap it about and see if he smells it. Buy another brown labradoodle, quickly.

I decided to do the second idea, but without the shouting. Doodle wouldn't come to me anyway. Why would he? I'd never ever shouted his name before. And I didn't want Bee to hear a mad boy (me) hollering her dog's name. No. No. Then I'd have to confess.

Doodle wasn't anywhere in the middle, so I headed for the edge of the park where there's a hedge all the way round. I'll try and explain how I felt inside. Sick. Scared. More sick. More scared. A picture of Doodle run over by a bus flashed onto the screen at the back of my eyeball. I blinked to delete it and took a deep breath. I needed to stay focused. Where would a dog go?

I didn't have the answer. But I could see someone who might. A dog owner with a small, white, fluffy dog, nothing like Doodle, but a dog's a dog, isn't it?

'I've lost my dog,' I said.

'Well I haven't got it,' he said. 'This is my dog.' He pulled the lead tight so the dog was virtually hanging off it and walked away sharpish, as though I was a dog-napper.

Oh no! Maybe Doodle had been dog-napped. I carried on jogging round the park, keeping next to the hedge. My heart was beating fast because of the exercise, making me feel more frightened. *BOOM BOOM BOOM BOOM BOOM.* It was like the music in a thriller when there's a murderer creeping towards the bedroom and someone's quivering under the duvet and there's no way out and no one's coming to help. (Not that I've ever watched a film like that.)

I saw a movement in the hedge. Phew! 'Doodle,' I said quietly – I didn't want him to run away.

The leaves vibrated again. I waited for him to poke his nose out. I wished I had some of those doggy treats that

Bee gives him. I held out my hand as though I did. *Good idea, Keener*, I thought.

'Doo-dle,' I said again, in a sing-songy way, like Fifty does when he talks to Probably Rose.

Out came the tip of his nose. It didn't look that familiar, but then I've never studied Doodle's nose. Out came the rest . . . of a squirrel.

GREYS VERSUS REDS

People think grey squirrels came into our country and stole all the food and chased away the nice red squirrels that already lived here. But they're wrong. And I'll tell you why (if I can remember everything that Jonno told me – he's the one who knows all this stuff).

Grey squirrels don't chase red ones. They can live together quite happily. But grey squirrels are better at surviving. They don't need as much food as red ones, and they don't get so many diseases. Loads of woodland has been chopped down so there's not as much food. It's nature. Greys are stronger. Greys eat less. Greys live. Reds die. Grey squirrels aren't 'tree rats', they're cute. Long live the greys!

More
Panic

I sat on the ground. I didn't know what to do. I knew I should tell Bee but I didn't want to. How do you tell someone you've lost their puppy? It's like telling someone's mum you've lost her baby or left them in the supermarket trolley. Or like telling Fifty you've lost his sister. That thought didn't help. He'd go ape. I'd be dead. No, I'd be tortured first. He'd devise a terrible ordeal for me, with ropes and winches and stretching and crowds of people cheering him on while I screamed. Like in Victorian times when criminals were hanged in the town square. Gross.

Daydreaming wasn't going to get Doodle back. I needed to act. But I stayed exactly where I was, because I didn't know what to do. What a mess! In the distance I thought I heard the burr of Marco's wheels. *Maybe he's got good news.*

A TYPICAL VICTORIAN FAMILY HAVING A CONVERSATION, MADE UP BY KEENER

Victorian mum: Let's have a day out and watch the hanging in the town square.

Victorian dad: Good idea. Shall we take the kids?

Victorian mum: Of course. They love a good hanging.

Victorian dad: Tell you what, let's take a picnic.

Victorian mum: Oh I can't wait. The children will be so excited.

I tried to focus my ears, but a second noise blanked out any trace of mountainboard. A much bigger sound. A siren. Coming this way. And coming fast. And maybe more than one. I forgot about Doodle for a second and wondered what the emergency was. And where it was. But it was literally only a second because suddenly two squad cars came into view, screeched to a tyre-burning halt right in front of me (if you exclude the grass between us) and out jumped three policemen.

It's amazing how many thoughts you can have one after the other. Here they are: *Something's wrong. It's odd that the police have arrived just as I've lost a dog, unless that's why the police are here. Is Doodle – I don't want to think it – dead? Did Doodle run into the street and cause a three-way pile up? The burr is getting louder. There's Marco. The police are coming this way. So is Marco. Marco's going very fast. They're on a collision course. Will they arrest me for losing the dog that caused the accident? Or for killing a dog? I need to go. I need to tell Bee. Marco can deal with the police. Or mow them down. Please don't let Doodle have been mown down.*

I jumped up and walked away, very fast. Away from Marco and away from the police, towards Bee and the picnic and the other Tribers. I didn't run, in case they chased me. My heart was pumping my blood around so quickly I could hear it. They were all where I'd left them: Bee, Copper Pie, Fifty, Jonno and . . . there was one more, Probably Rose. *Why was she there? Who cares?* My brain could only deal with the dog thing. I blurted out the awful news before I even got to them. 'I've lost Doodle. I'm really sorry.'

Everyone's heads snapped round and fixed on me with confused expressions as though they thought it was a joke, or they'd heard wrong.

'What did you say, Keener?' Bee was on her feet, ready for 'fight or flight'. (We learnt that in science. It's how we're programmed to react to danger – either run away or attack. I hoped she wasn't going to attack me.) I had to swallow a couple of times because something was blocking my talking pipe. 'Marco had the lead round his foot,' I said. 'I went off

24

on the mountainboard. When I came back, Doodle was gone.' (I felt bad about dishing the dirt on Marco, but it was the truth.) Jonno got to his feet too. They both stared at me as I finished off what I had to say. 'And the police are here, and . . .' *And what?* I didn't have anything else to say. I pointed in the vague direction of the police and Marco.

'And what?' said Jonno.

'I don't know.' I could feel tears trying to force their way over my bottom eyelid, but I held them back. I had the feeling Bee could read my thoughts. Maybe she could even see the picture in my head of Doodle, flattened, hedgehog-style.

She raced off, running across the park with Jonno right behind. Copper Pie went too. I stayed where I was, with Fifty and Rose (who was *covered* in chocolate cake). Fifty screwed up his face. I think he was deciding what to say. Rose smiled at me, but I couldn't smile back. She pushed some mushed chocolate cake towards her mouth. Some of it fell on her polo shirt, right on top of where it said *Blue Skies Nursery*.

'What's she doing here?' I asked.

'She was in the play area, but she wanted to come with me, didn't you, Rose?'

'I thought she was at nursery.'

'She was. They brought all the nursery kids to the park.'

'Oh.' I didn't care about Rose. She wasn't lost, not like Doodle. Fifty read my mind. A lot of that goes on with the

Tribers. It's helpful if you don't have to explain everything all the time.

'Don't worry,' he said. 'Dogs get lost every day. Think of all the posters you see on lampposts.'

I did. It didn't help. 'The posters are always for cats, not dogs. Dogs don't get lost because they're meant to be on a lead.'

'Good point,' said Fifty. 'Does Doodle have a collar?'

'What do you think the lead was attached to?' I said.

Fifty ignored my sarky voice. 'So, the collar will say Doodle's name and address. He's probably at home already.'

A bit of hope made its way into my clogged-with-doom brain. 'Do you think so?' He nodded, so I dared to ask the other question that was worrying me. 'So why are the police here?'

'Maybe Doodle was spotted in the road and someone rang them?' said Fifty. I thought about that. It seemed possible. 'Or maybe Doodle bit someone's ankle and they reported him?' That was his second suggestion. I thought about that too. 'Or maybe Doodle stole a picnic, or some shoes. He likes gnawing shoes.' I stared at my fellow Triber to make sure he was taking it seriously. He seemed to be.

'So you don't think Doodle's been run over?'

'No way,' said Fifty. 'He's too fast.'

I was beginning to feel better. There was no evidence that anything terrible had happened to Doodle. I helped myself to a chocolate cake, took a bite and nearly didn't manage to swallow it because out of the corner of my eye I saw shapes coming towards us. I rotated to move them from my peripheral vision onto the main screen. Two of the three police officers were heading our way.

I moved the piece of chocolate cake around inside my mouth trying to break it down into swallowable pieces.

They came closer. Walking side by side.

I looked at Fifty. He was messing about with Probably Rose. I wanted to tell him, but the chocolate cake was in the way. I needed saliva to make it squidgy, but there didn't seem to be any.

I risked another look, hoping they'd altered their course. Nope. They were coming for us, for definite, and Copper Pie was behind them. Whatever it was, it wasn't good.

Confession
Time

I decided to speak first. I reckoned there was a better chance of not being arrested if I admitted guilt right away. As I opened my mouth to begin, Copper Pie shook his head from side to side. It was a message, obviously, but I didn't know what it meant, so I ignored it.

'I did it,' I said. 'It was me. I —'

'Stop right there, lad,' said the extremely tall policeman. (The other one was actually a woman). I stopped. And waited. He looked at me, then Fifty, then Rose. I couldn't stand the not knowing. What was going on? Why hadn't Bee and Jonno come back with Copper Pie? Were they cradling Doodle's head while he took his last breath?

'Please, what's going on?' I said in a desperate voice.

'Calm down, lad.' The big man spoke again. 'There's no

hurry. We can see that now.' Quite what he could 'see now' from looking at our picnic I didn't know. He turned and nodded at the policewoman who walked off and said something muffled into her bleeping radio. The big one carried on, 'We just need to get to the bottom of this situation.' He patted me on the shoulder. I didn't want to be patted. I wanted to know what was going on. Did 'no hurry' mean it was too late? Was Doodle dead? In my head the idea that I'd killed Bee's dog was fizzing like a bottle of lemonade about to explode.

It exploded. 'Have you found him? Is he hurt? Is he DEAD?' I shouted.

Copper Pie made a shut-up-idiot face but I couldn't. *I am a murderer*, I thought.

The policewoman stepped forwards and patted my other shoulder. *Stop all this patting*, I wanted to shout, but I didn't.

'Is who dead?' she asked in an I'm-trying-to-be-kind voice.

'Doodle.' As I said his name out loud (even though it wasn't very loud), I felt a flood of tears spill.

'They're not here about Doodle, idiot,' said Copper Pie.

What! It took a while to sink in. The police weren't here because of Doodle. *Phew!* All the bubbles went out of the lemonade in my head.

'But maybe we should be,' said the big policeman. 'Who exactly is Doodle?'

Fifty stood up and sighed dramatically, as though he was surrounded by morons. He explained it all to the police officers in a nursery-teacher voice. 'Doodle is Bee's dog. Keener took the dog over the other side of the park and gave him to Marco. Marco lost him. Keener is worried that the dog's dead. But I think he's probably run home. So we're going to go and look for him.' Fifty sat back down and started packing up the picnic food.

'Not just yet you're not,' said the big one. 'Now . . . who might this be?' He pointed at Rose. She smiled at him. The whole of the bottom half of her face was chocolate brown.

'That's my sister,' said Fifty.

The big one stared at Copper Pie. 'You didn't say there was a little girl with you.'

'She wasn't with me, she was with *him*.' Copper Pie pointed at Fifty.

'You need to watch yourself, boy. Now, what might this little girl's name be?'

'Probably Rose,' said Copper Pie.

'Don't you be funny with me, *laddie*. She's either Rose or she isn't.' He was cross, very. Copper Pie looked a bit scared. I thought I'd better help.

'Her parents couldn't decide what to call her. So every time someone asked, they said "She's probably Rose".'

The police officer looked like he wanted to strangle someone.

'But who actually took her?' said the woman.

And before we could answer the big one snapped, 'Out with it – which one of you is the kidnapper?'

30

Kidnap

What was he talking about? There was no kidnapper. And no kidnapped. I had a crazy thought. *Maybe they weren't police at all. Maybe they were nutters in fancy dress.* I snuck a peek at the uniforms to see if they looked real. They did. And I had seen the cop cars with my own eyes. (I said it was a crazy idea.)

The lady spoke again. 'We know it was one of you, so you'd better tell us. The sooner we know what happened, the sooner it gets put right.'

If they'd asked me to confess to the dog-killing I'd have blurted it out no problem, but kidnapping? Nope. Not me.

Rose made a mewing sound. (If she wanted more cake all she had to do was lick her face.) Fifty went to pick her up but the big policeman stepped over to the rug and said, 'We'll leave her there, I think.'

Fifty didn't like that. 'If I want to pick up my own sister, I will.'

'She's quite happy where she is.' You could tell by the way the policeman spoke that what he really meant was DO AS I SAY! But Fifty either didn't get it or didn't care, because he bent over and picked up Rose anyway. And that's when he repeated what he'd said to me at our biscuit breakfast.

'I don't know why you're here, but if you upset Probably Rose, you'll have *me* to deal with.'

The policeman didn't like Fifty's tone. He was about to be mashed. Luckily the policewoman stepped between the two of them before anything happened. 'Let's calm this down.'

'I am calm,' said Fifty. (Red face, gritted teeth.)

Unlike Fifty, I *was* actually calm, but only because I knew no Triber was ever going to be a kidnapper. I mean, we're kids. It was all a mistake.

'You're going to have to confess in the end, but for now why don't I tell you something?' said the policewoman. 'A little girl has been reported missing. She was in the play area with a lot of other children from the Blue Skies Nursery. They were about to head back when they noticed she wasn't there. A missing child is a *very* serious incident.'

As I heard the words and strung them together to hear them again in my head I couldn't believe that I'd been so stupid. There was a kidnap. And a kidnapper. And I knew *exactly* who he was.

My Friend Is Completely and Utterly Mental

'I didn't kidnap her. You can't kidnap your own sister,' shouted Fifty.

'You took her from the play area without permission when she was in the care of the nursery,' said the police woman. 'That's kidnap. On top of which you've caused a lot of distress, and wasted our time.'

'It was Rose who was distressed. And if they were looking after her, how come I walked into the play area and chatted to her and brought her out here without anyone noticing?' Fifty, my small friend who usually avoids trouble, stared straight up at the two police officers. 'How come?'

It just shows you how much he loves his sister. Nothing else would have made him so brave, or reckless, or completely and utterly mental. I held my breath, waiting for the handcuffs. Copper Pie put his head in his hands. The Tribe picnic really wasn't going that well – a lost dog, a Triber about to be arrested, Probably Rose drowning in chocolate mush, and Bee and Jonno scouring the streets for Doodle (I assumed that's where they were).

'I don't like your attitude, laddie.' The big one stepped round the policewoman to be closer to Fifty.

'I don't care. You're not taking my sister.'

Watching Fifty being ruder and ruder made me realise I had to do something before he was thrown in the back of the cop car and never seen again. Fifty's just not logical when it comes to Rose. I took a deep breath, but I was still full of the last one so I coughed, and accidentally spat out some cake – a bit of brown sludge landed on the big policeman's black trousers.

'Fifty, they won't take Rose anywhere. Just tell them what you did. Tell them . . .' I forgot for a second that I was trying to get him out of trouble and let rip. '. . . tell them that you're a complete idiot and you should never have taken Rose from the play area. I bet she wasn't even upset – you just didn't want her to go back to Blue Skies. It's not normal to make such a fuss about a toddler going to nursery. We all went.' I stopped. Even though I hadn't meant to say what I really thought, it seemed to work. Fifty didn't look mad any more, he looked . . . wobbly, like he might cry or faint or wail.

'She did look a *bit* sad,' he said quietly, eyes firmly fixed

on the ground. 'She was sitting on the grass doing nothing.'
I didn't point out that there's not an awful lot you can do
when you're not even two years old. She was hardly going
to be reading the paper or playing Mario on her DS.

The third policeman appeared from the direction of the
play area. 'So, here's the missing Rose, I see.' He smiled. He
was obviously the nice cop in the good cop/bad cop routine.
It must have been him that the policewoman bleeped with
her radio when she saw Rose with her Blue Skies polo shirt
on. 'You gave those nursery girls a fright. They thought
they'd lost her. Searched the playground, then called us.
They're all in tears, even though it's all over. Good job we
bumped into your friends or there'd have been a whole heap
of trouble.' That didn't make any sense to me. Or to Copper
Pie.

'But we didn't know Rose was missing,' he said. 'We
thought you were looking for the missing dog.'

'Yes, but when I asked you who else you were with,' the
policeman stared straight at Copper Pie, 'one of the names
you said was "Thomas Baines".' It was odd hearing Fifty's
real name. No one uses it.

'And the missing girl was Rose Baines,' I said, working it
out aloud.

'So we thought the missing girl just *might* be with her
brother.'

Everyone looked at Fifty, who had stopped looking like
an angry pit bull terrier and now looked more like a lost

puppy. (I wished I hadn't had that thought. It reminded me about Doodle.)

'I'm very sorry,' he said. 'And I suppose . . . nursery wasn't really that bad.'

TRIBERS' BEST NURSERY MEMORIES

KEENER: The mattresses they put out after lunch in the quiet room for napping.

COPPER PIE: Scaring everybody by hanging upside-down on the monkey bars.

FIFTY: The water toy outside, with canal boats and a system of gates and locks.

BEE: Making an Advent calendar out of boxes from the junk pile that was bigger than her. In each box she wrote a message that no one could read because she hadn't learnt to write yet.

JONNO: Everything at his Montessori nursery was kid-sized. Ace.

'Am I in big, big trouble?' said Fifty with his best puppy-dog eyes.

The Verdict

We waited to hear what the three police officers would say.

'Shall we leave it to you, Sarge?' said the policewoman.

'Yes,' said the nice one. 'I can handle this lot.'

'We'll be off then,' said the scary one. *Phew!* 'Try and keep out of trouble, you lot. We don't want to see you again. Do you hear?'

The three of us nodded. Rose noticed, so she did it too. That would normally have made Fifty go over the top about how great she is, but he stayed quiet. *Good move.*

'OK.' Our nice policeman sat down on the rug. 'I'm Sergeant Farrow. Or Rob as most people call me, except the ones in handcuffs.' He laughed. I wanted to laugh too but didn't think I should. 'Looks tasty,' he said, looking at what was left on the picnic rug.

'Would you like a cake?' said Fifty.

'I would.' He reached out and took the last one. Rose mewed again.

'She's a cute little bundle,' said Sergeant Farrow.

'She's really clever,' said Fifty.

'Doesn't take after her brother, then.' He winked.

'I didn't think,' said Fifty. 'I never would have taken her if I'd thought they'd call the police.'

Idiot, I thought. *They were hardly going to go back to the Blue Skies Nursery minus one child, were they?*

'Well, you and I had better take Rose over to the play area so she can go back to the nursery with the others.'

Fifty nodded. Maybe he was in the clear – not arrested, not even a warning. It was brilliant that Rose was found, not that we knew she was missing, but what about Doodle? I needed a genie to grant me a wish.

WAYS TO MAKE A WISH
(no guarantee offered)

- Throw money in a well.
- Win a wishbone battle (chicken required).
- Blow dandelion seeds.
- Catch a falling leaf (or a star, but that's unlikely).
- Blow out birthday candles (but not someone else's).
- Find a genie.

Fifty's Kidnap

Or maybe I just needed a policeman. Sergeant Farrow finished the cake, brushed the crumbs off his lap and stood up. I had to say something before he went away.

'There's another problem.' I could feel the usual rosy glow of embarrassment creeping up my cheeks. I carried on anyway. 'The problem I thought you were here about.' He waited for me to go on. 'The dog. He's lost.'

'Ahh!' said the nice policeman. He turned towards Copper Pie. 'The girl you were with earlier, she mentioned her dog was gone.'

'That's right,' said Copper Pie.

I waited to hear what the plan was. It was great knowing we had an adult to help. And not just an ordinary adult – a sergeant with three stripes on his shoulder.

'I wouldn't worry. I expect he'll turn up. Pets usually do.'

I couldn't believe what he'd said. I repeated it in my head. It didn't get any better. He was leaving it to us. He cared about missing babies, but not missing dogs. Missing dogs could form a pack and eat stray kittens, terrorise old ladies by barking at their thick brown tights, be made into burgers – it didn't matter to him.

So that meant one thing and one thing only – Tribe was on its own. I thought back to all the amazing things we'd done since we became Tribe and knew that the only way to get Doodle back safely was for the Tribers to work together. I started shoving everything into my rucksack.

'I've got to go. I've got to find Bee and Jonno, and then

39

we've got to find Doodle. Are you coming, Copper Pie?'

'Yep.'

'I'll see you later,' said Fifty. 'I'd better . . .' He tilted his head to one side.

'Tribehouse,' said Copper Pie.

'What time?' said Fifty.

I checked my watch. It was bang on twelve o'clock. 'Three o'clock.' That gave us plenty of time to scout around for dog tracks before heading over to Tribe HQ in Fifty's garden, hopefully with Doodle trotting along with us. Making a plan of action made me feel better. I had Copper Pie by my side. A belly full of food. And a job to do.

I was ready.

The Tribe
Ideas Machine

We didn't have to look very hard for Bee and Jonno. We left the park heading towards the café and saw them coming back towards us. No dog. I was a bit worried Bee would blank me, I mean it was all my fault, but she just shrugged.

'No luck, then,' said Copper Pie.

'Nope,' said Jonno. 'But we've only done school and the alley.'

'So where next?' said Copper Pie.

Bee shook her head.

'I know it seems hopeless. He could be anywhere. But we've got to keep looking, haven't we?' said Jonno.

She nodded. I felt really bad. I tried to think of something that might cheer her up. If only the policeman had offered to help. With the siren on, *nee naw nee naw*, they could have raced around the streets in no time.

'OK,' said Jonno. 'Let's have one of Fifty's brainstorms and see if we can think of any better way to find Doodle.'

Fifty taught us how to do them. There are rules. We can say whatever we like but no one's allowed to criticise. No 'that's rubbish' or 'it won't work'. The idea is that if you know no one is going to make fun of you, your imagination works better. The trouble with Tribe brainstorms, though, is that we end up with a list of crazy ideas and no answers. But we keep trying.

'I'm in,' said Bee.

Copper Pie nodded.

'OK,' I said. *You never know,* I thought. *This could be the one time it works.* We sat down on the grass: me, Bee, Copper Pie and Jonno. And looked at each other. I was really hot. Everyone says we have rubbish summers but it hadn't rained for ages. I know because it's my job to water Mum's rockery when it looks dry, and that's every day. I helped her make it, lugging all the rocks, and she planted it. Bet nothing will grow. Mum's fingers are green – it's just a pity they're arsenic green.

Bee sighed, swished her fringe out of her eyes and started us off. 'Doodle likes food. He'd head for food.'

That was it – we were off, Tribe style.

'The butchers.'

'There isn't one round here.'

KILLER WALLPAPER

Wallpaper used to be dyed green using arsenic. If the room was damp the arsenic produced a gas that killed people. So children with green bedrooms were more likely to die than children with blue or red, or in fact any other colour bedrooms. (Don't worry if your room's green. They don't use it any more.)

'The supermarket then.'

'It's quite a way from the park.'

'And smells of plastic, not food.'

'Shoe shops.'

'Dogs don't wear shoes.'

'He chews them.'

'Bone shops. He chews bones.'

'What about pet shops?'

'Does he like fish?'

'Only cooked.'

I'm sure you get the idea. Our brainstorms just don't work. I zoned out and tried to imagine what Doodle would do, let off his lead for the first time in his short life. It was difficult. Dogs walk on four legs, not two. Dogs don't use knives and forks. Dogs poo wherever they want, not in toilets. Dogs don't wipe. I was wondering whether Doodle's idea of family was the same as a human's when

Bee called a halt to the list of unhelpful suggestions.

'It's no good. We're not going to find Doodle sitting here. And if I go home without him Mum'll have a fit. So we may as well walk.'

Bee had spoken. She's boss. We all stood up.

Telephone
Numbers

Bee walked fast (only stopping to collect litter).

'Doodle,' she shouted. 'Doodle!'

Jonno did the same. 'Doodle!'

So did Copper Pie. 'Doodle!'

Oh well, I thought, and joined in. 'Doodle!'

We decided to use the telephone method to choose our route. It seemed as good a way as any of finding a runaway labradoodle.

On the way C.P. and I filled Bee and Jonno in on the 'kidnap'.

Bee was shocked. 'Imagine the trouble Fifty'd have been in if they hadn't found her.'

Walking was dull. We finished Copper Pie's phone number, which he couldn't remember but I could, quite

THE TELEPHONE NUMBER METHOD OF GOING FOR A WALK

Pick a telephone number, e.g. 358179. Take left and right turns based on the order of the numbers, ignoring any zeros. So . . .

- Take the 3rd right.
- Take the 5th left.
- Take the 8th right.
- Take the 1st left.
- Take the 7th right.
- Take the 9th left.

near Fifty's road so we decided to go to the Tribehouse early. We were meant to be meeting Fifty at 3 p.m. It was 2.42 p.m. Doodle had been missing for four hours.

Fifty was there already. I asked him if Rose was OK. He nodded. I asked him if he was OK. He nodded. Fifty is usually talkative. I asked him if his mum knew about the kidnap. He nodded. That explained it.

'I went back to the Blue Skies Nursery with Rose. The policeman came too. They called Mum from there and she came and picked us both up.'

'Was she cross?'

'Not really. She was how she *always* is.'

'What do you mean?' said Jonno. I didn't need to ask, but Jonno's only been at our school for less than a term so there's still stuff he doesn't know. (Although we're teaching him, using the famous, and funny, Tribe fact files that we keep in the safe in the Tribehouse with titles like *Things Tribers Are Scared Of* and *Tribers' Embarrassing Moments*.)

'Whenever I do anything wrong, instead of a straight-forward telling off, I get "quality time" with Mum. If anything goes wrong, she thinks it's her fault because she hasn't "parented" me properly. I'd rather have a few swishes of the cane. But no, I get days and days of me-and-mummy chats.' Fifty sighed.

'I don't think I've ever been parented,' said Bee with a small grin. It was the first smile since she found out Doodle was gone. It soon disappeared.

'Lucky you. Being parented is like being in a zoo – she watches me all the time, checking for weird behaviours.'

'Like what?' said Jonno.

'Twitching, rocking backwards and forwards, maybe dribbling,' said Fifty. He demonstrated and rolled his eyes at the same time. It was funny.

'You're mean,' said Bee. (She really likes Fifty's mum.) 'Your mum's nice. She's just a bit too . . . involved in your life.'

'She thinks I'm "too fond" of Rose.' Fifty's face looked really serious. 'How can you be "too fond" of your sister?'

Good question, I thought. But I had a better one. *How can you be 'fond' of your sister at all?* Sisters are not my favourite thing.

TRIBERS' BROTHERS AND SISTERS

KEENER: One small, irritating sister, Flo, and one big, irritating sister, Amy.

COPPER PIE: Little brother, Charlie, who he tortures and calls 'Snot'.

JONNO: Doesn't have any, would like one (but why?).

BEE: Two brothers (twins), about 20, who live with an actress in Stoke Park.

FIFTY: One precious, clever, marvellous, fantastic, awesome sister (he thinks).

There was a bit of a silence and then Fifty stood up (he was sitting on the safe – his usual spot) and showed us the piece of paper he'd been keeping warm under his butt. It was a poster. There was a drawing of a dog in the middle and a great big heading: *HELP, WE'VE LOST DOODLE.*

'It's what people do when they lose cats,' he said.

Bee said, 'Thanks, that's great.' I was glad she'd spoken because I was trying not to laugh at the two-legged swollen-headed sheep crossed with a rabbit that was meant to be Doodle. No chance of anyone recognising Bee's labradoodle from *that* picture.

'We'll need more,' said Jonno. 'One for every lamppost.'

'No problem,' said Fifty. 'I wanted to show you before I made copies.'

'We should add where and when he was lost and a phone number to call,' I said.

Fifty added all the details at the bottom. I was glad I'd said something useful to show Bee how much I wanted to get Doodle back.

'Anything else?' We shook our heads. Fifty disappeared. Jonno winked at us all. We all winked back.

'It didn't look anything like my dog,' said Bee.

'It didn't look like a dog. Full stop,' said Jonno.

'Looked more like a chicken with ears,' said Copper Pie.

Bee put her finger on her lips – we didn't want Fifty to hear us.

'Couldn't we get a photo instead?' I said.

'Not without going to my house,' said Bee. 'Without a dog.' *Good point.*

'What else can we do?' said Jonno. 'Posters are great but there must be more.'

'We could check Doodle's not gone home?' I said.

Bee made a face. 'Same problem. How do I do that without letting Mum know what's happened?'

'I could ring,' I said. 'If Doodle had arrived home without you your mum would tell me, wouldn't she?' I didn't want to volunteer, but it was *all* my fault.

'There's no point,' said Jonno. 'If Doodle arrived home

on his own, Bee's mum would be worried and ring Bee straight away.'

Bee checked her mobile. 'No missed calls.'

No one had any other ideas – well, not to do with the dog anyway.

'Is there any grub in the biscuit tin?' asked Copper Pie (he's always hungry), as Fifty came back in clutching a big pile of paper.

'Nope,' said Fifty. 'But you can come up to the house. Mum saw the poster on the printer. She wants to talk to us.'

I was quite pleased. Having a grown-up in the know made it seem more likely Doodle would be found. We walked up the garden and in the kitchen door. Fifty's mum was sitting at the table – with no music on, which was unusual. Bee dumped all the rubbish she'd found in the kitchen bin.

'So, Tribe is busy these days,' she said as we filed in. 'Not content with stealing my daughter, you've also managed to lose Bee's dog.' She was joking but none of us laughed. She made us sound horrible. When we formed Tribe we decided we'd be loyal and fair, and not a gang that didn't like other kids and were mean and stuff. I felt really bad. Everything we'd done before had turned out fine, but this time we'd really messed up. *I'd* really messed up. I waited to hear what else she was going to say. And while I waited I wondered whether, if we didn't find Doodle, could we still be Tribe? If we never saw Doodle again, could Bee still be my friend?

Doodle's
Army

Half an hour later we were back on the streets, posters and drawing pins in our hands. But there weren't five of us any more. There were ten. Fifty's mum said we needed help, so that's what we got (or she got to be exact). She rang Fifty's dad and he came straight home from his post round rather than going to the gym. She wanted to ask Bee's mum and dad, but we begged her not to say anything until we'd had one more really good look for Doodle. She agreed, a bit reluctantly. Fifty's dad rang Copper Pie's dad on the way home and he came straight round with Charlie (and luckily agreed that Bee's mum didn't need to know just yet). (Nobody suggested we ring my mum – she'd have shopped us to Bee's mum immediately. And no one really knows Jonno's parents yet.) So, there were the five Tribers, Fifty's mum and dad and Rose, Copper Pie's dad and Charlie. We were Doodle's army.

At the end of the road we split up into three teams. I went with Copper Pie, his dad and Charlie – because Charlie asked me too. (He likes me because I'm the only one who makes marble runs for him to play with.) Every team had a route and a batch of posters. Doodle couldn't hide from all of us. No way.

The Invisible Dog

We left Fifty's house at half-past three. We started off walking really fast and chatting and laughing and stuff, but by the time we'd been up and down street after street we got slower and talked less and the only one of us with any enthusiasm was Charlie who said, 'There's Doodle' every time he saw a dog, a cat, a woodpigeon, a wheelie bin or a garden gnome. He also said it every time he saw a hedge or a bush and dived under to have a look. At first it was funny, then it got irritating and by the time we got back to Fifty's we all hated him. (And I'm never making a marble run for him ever again.) We kept in contact with the other groups on the way round. No one had good news. My feet were hurting and I wanted to go home. I was thirsty too.

POINTLESS OR IMPORTANT OR WEIRD TRIBERS' FACTS (AND ONE LIE)

KEENER: If you feel thirsty you're already getting dehydrated.

JONNO: In a lifetime, the average person eats 70 spiders while they're asleep.

COPPER PIE: David Beckham, Cristiano Ronaldo and Copper Pie all wore the number 7 shirt at Man Utd. (This is not a fact. This is a daydream.)

FIFTY: Most breakfast cereals contain more sugar than doughnuts.

BEE: An area of rainforest the size of a football-pitch is destroyed every second.

Before we all went off to our own homes we had a Tribe-plus-friends debrief in the road outside Fifty's. Fifty's dad was in charge, with Copper Pie's dad chipping in. It went like this.

Fifty's dad: It's six o'clock. Time to get some food inside us, I think. Try not to worry, Bee. We're a nation of dog lovers – someone will find Doodle.

C.P.'s dad: Too right.

Fifty's dad: The day's not over yet. A dog on the loose will be more noticeable in the evening. He may get brought back at any time.

C.P.'s dad: Right again.

Fifty's dad: Go home, Bee. Whoever finds him will read his tag and call.

Charlie: Five free free six one nuffing seven.

Fifty's dad: What did he say?

C.P.'s dad: Ignore him, he's a pest. Aren't you Charlie? (Charlie nodded, smiling. He never realises he's being insulted.)

Charlie: Number five free free six one nuffing seven.

Bee: That's my phone number. How come you know it, Charlie?

(Charlie put his hand in his pocket. He pulled out a blue dog tag. It looked a lot like Doodle's blue dog tag.)

C.P.'s dad: Where did you get that?

Charlie: In the bush.

Fifty's dad: What bush?

The rest of the conversation consisted of the dads demanding Charlie identify which bush and Charlie shaking his head. (He is only three.)

It had all got worse. Doodle had lost his tag, so even if he was found no one would know where he lived. The only hope was that the posters of the sheeprabbitchicken worked, or Doodle smelt his way back home.

Bee's ringtone blared out of her pocket. 'Oh no, it's Mum!' she said.

'You've got to answer it,' said Jonno. 'But you don't have to tell.'

Bee's mum wanted her home for tea. Bee looked terrified. She went even paler and her eyes looked too large for her face. She asked Jonno to go with her. And that was the end of Doodle's army. Bee and Jonno went off together. Everyone else drifted away.

What a terrible day, a kidnap and a lost dog. If only I'd stayed with the Tribers instead of going husky-boarding. I'd have made Fifty take Rose back straightaway and I wouldn't have lost the dog. Everything was my fault.

Flat On My Face

I lay in bed, wide awake. It was like someone was still screening short films onto the back of my eye, films about Doodle. Doodle drowned. Doodle in pieces. Doodle run over. Doodle in a bin liner. I abandoned bed and tried my hammock, and that must have worked because I had a dream about being on a sailing boat. There was a wave coming and it turned the boat over and I landed flat on my face on my bedroom carpet, with a bit of Lego pressed into my cheek. Not a great way to start the day.

I checked my phone straight away, hoping for a message from Bee with a smiley face at the end. Nope. No messages from anyone. It was 7.14 a. m. *What to do?*

I got back in my hammock and swayed for a bit. Usually I like being on my own, but that morning, swinging from side to side worrying about Doodle, I didn't like it at all. I even thought about going to get the evil Flo up. Thankfully Mum came in.

'You're up early,' she said.

I grunted. Why do mums say stuff you already know?

'I spoke to Bee's mum last night,' she said.

I grunted again. This time it was because I was scared about what was coming next.

'She was quite upset.'

I could work that out for myself. I grunted again.

'I'm not working today, so I said we'd join the search party this morning.'

That deserved more than a grunt. I said, 'OK.'

'Bee's mum said they were going out for another look last night. Poor things, scouring the streets in the dark.' Mum sighed.

I grunted again. It's much easier than using words when you don't know what to say.

'I'm going to wake Amy. She asked me to make sure she was up to help. So, breakfast and then we'll be off.' Mum headed for the door. 'Flo's ready, and she's clutching her loudspeaker!'

I smiled. I wasn't on my own. My family was helping. I needed to get up and get going, like Mum said.

By 7.45 a. m. we were fed and teeth-cleaned. We walked over to Bee's with Flo talking all the way through her loud-speaker. Luckily the batteries were dead.

'Will they buy another dog if they can't find Doodle?'

'Do dogs eat birds?'

'Does anything eat dogs?'

'Do dogs get toothache?'

'If they get another dog, will that be called Doodle too?'

Mum did all the answering. Amy was sleepwalking – it was early for her, but she was coming, which was amazing. First nice thing I could ever remember her doing. I walked behind, practising positive thinking. Fifty's mum says if you can picture what you want in your head, you're more likely to get it. It's nonsense of course, but I did it anyway. I made images of Doodle racing along, his ears flying out behind him. Doodle jumping up at Bee. Doodle dragging me at high speed on Marco's board. In a way it worked. Doodle was so real in my head, he couldn't possibly be dead.

It was quiet, as though the whole world was on school holiday. Maybe everyone had taken Friday off like my mum? We didn't see one single other person until a car slowed down by the side of us, a police car, and a familiar head leant out. It was Sergeant Farrow.

'Hello again,' he said.

Mum gave me a funny look. Not surprising – policemen don't usually speak to me. She didn't know about the kidnap, so she probably thought I'd been caught spraying graffiti. (She probably didn't. I mean, this is Keener speaking.)

'Hi,' I said.

'Nice morning for a walk,' he said, and drove off, leaving me with a nosy mum. I told her all about it. It's not as though *I'd* done anything wrong.

'Would you come and kidnap me if I was sad?' asked Flo.

Not in a million years, I thought. 'Maybe,' I said.

Copper Pie and Jonno were waiting outside Bee's

'Shall we go in?' said Mum.

'There's no answer,' said Jonno.

'Bee's dad's car's not there,' said Copper Pie.

'He'll be at work,' said Mum. She walked up to the door and knocked three times. (The bell doesn't work.) Nothing. We looked at each other in the way people do when no one knows what's going on.

'There's Fifty,' said Jonno. Flo gave him a wave.

'Where's Bee?' he said.

'No idea,' said Jonno. 'It's weird because last night she asked me to come over this morning.'

'Same,' said Fifty.

'Let's try the kitchen door,' I said. That's the way Bee always goes in. Mum hung behind – I think she thought it was rude going round the back. Fifty stayed talking to Flo. Copper Pie rapped on the back door, really hard. We waited. Still nothing.

'Shall we call her?' said Jonno. *Good idea.* He got his phone out. Held it to his ear for a while.

'Hello,' said Jonno. 'Bee?'

The person at the other end must have spoken.

'We're outside.'

The person at the other end must have spoken again.

'OK,' said Jonno, and ended the call. 'She's coming to let us in,' he said. 'She was asleep.'

Bee came to the back door wrapped in a brown, fluffy dressing gown that went all the way to her feet. She looked like a brown bear.

'Sorry,' she said, rubbing her eyes. 'We stayed up really late. We were looking for Doodle everywhere. It was after midnight when we got back.'

Bee's mum appeared. She looked like a bear too, a bigger black one, but with red eyes.

'Oh, the Tribers.' She put her hand on Bee's shoulder. 'Your lovely friends. Thank you. Thank you.' She looked like she was going to cry. 'We've overslept.'

It was a bit awkward standing outside the door with Bee and her mum talking to us in their dressing gowns, all upset and teary-looking.

'Shall we come back later?' said Jonno. 'We'll look for Doodle on our own . . . and come back later.' *Well done. Jonno.*

Bee looked at her mum. 'OK, thanks.' She shut the door. We walked back round to the front and told Mum.

'I expect they're exhausted,' she said. 'Never mind. We can search without them – go to the park and a few other places. You never know.' Mum used a cheery voice but I didn't feel very cheery. Bee's family had looked all last night. We'd looked all day. The chances of finding Doodle were zero.

'OK,' said Jonno.

'Same,' said Fifty.

'Why do you always say "same"?' asked Flo, through the loudspeaker. She didn't care that it didn't work.

'Because I always agree with the other Tribers.' Fifty smiled and put out his fist. Copper Pie, Jonno and I made fists too and we all banged knuckles in the Tribe fist of friendship, but didn't feel as good as normal.

Mum and Amy and Flo and Fifty headed off. I dawdled behind with Jonno and Copper Pie in silence. I heard a car coming. We were about to cross over the road, so I checked behind and saw it was a police car. Mum always says if you see a police car you should step right over to the far side of the pavement or onto the grass if there is any. She says policemen race around and kill more pedestrians than they save. (That probably isn't true.) She also says you should never stand on the hard shoulder of the motorway – you should climb up the bank, or whatever's there, or a lorry will mow you down. (I'm not sure how useful that information is to an eleven-year-old who can't drive for another six years.)

'Police car,' I shouted, to warn the others. Everyone stopped. Mum took her own advice and pressed her back against a garden wall, leaving her two daughters to be flattened (only joking). We all watched the car drive, incredibly slowly, towards us.

'Must be a learner,' said Copper Pie.

I would have laughed but I was too busy staring at the driver, and the passenger, and what looked like a third head between the two people in the front seat. The sun was in my eyes making it difficult to work out what was face and what was shadow. I squinted to see if that helped. It did. The police car drew up by my side. I didn't wait for the police to get out. I grabbed the handle and flung open the back door.

Doodle's Sleepover

Doodle leapt out of the car. He bypassed me even though I was the closest, and jumped all over Jonno (his best friend after Bee). Jonno pretty much jumped all over Doodle too.

The passenger door opened and out stepped our favourite policeman ever, the nice one from the day before, the one and only Sergeant Farrow.

'Hello again,' he said.

'Hello,' I said. 'You've got Bee's dog.'

'Bright boy,' he said. 'Nearly as bright as your kidnapper friend over there.' He nodded at Fifty. Fifty waved back. (There was something about Sergeant Farrow that reminded me of Copper Pie's neighbour, Big Jim. He jokes about things, rather than being serious like most adults.)

Mum came over. 'Hello, I understand you've met my son and his friends.'

'Yes,' he said. 'I was lucky enough to run into them yesterday. A small matter of a missing person.' He raised his eyebrows. Good job I'd told Mum.

'I heard,' she said. 'I hope it didn't cause too much trouble.'

'Actually, the boys gave me a cake so I decided to let them off.' He winked at me. Mum talked to him for a few minutes. Gradually everyone gathered round, waiting for her to ask the question that we all wanted the answer to. (Doodle stayed right by Jonno's side, as though he didn't want to get lost again.) In the end, it was Flo who butted in. Typical.

'Where did you find Doodle, please?' she said, through the loudspeaker of course.

'He came with our breakfast,' said Sergeant Farrow, grinning. 'Not long after we saw you, in fact.'

'Really?' said Flo, eyes popping out of her head. I think she thought Doodle had served the policeman a full English wearing an apron.

'Sort of,' he said.

'Please tell us,' said Jonno.

Sergeant Farrow could see we were all desperate to hear the full story. 'You know the café with the tattoo parlour at the back?'

We all nodded. There aren't many cafés where you can get a cappuccino and a scorpion down your neck at the same time.

'Well, we go there for our bacon butties. But this morning, Toni, the owner, had a surprise for us. Doodle turned up last night as he was closing. There was no tag on him, but Toni recognised him, said he belonged to a girl with a long, black fringe and a boy with frizzy hair and glasses. So he locked him up in the back with a tasty meal and a bowl of water.'

'Like a sleepover,' said Flo.

'Exactly like a sleepover.' He really was a nice policeman.

'When we turned up this morning Toni handed him over. And of course we knew *exactly* who he was talking about.'

TONI'S DESCRIPTIONS
OF THE TRIBERS

Frizzy-haired boy with glasses, clever-looking – Jonno.

Little boy with curly black hair, needs more food – Fifty.

Bossy girl with the long, black fringe in her eyes – Bee.

Quiet one, blond, likes bacon sandwiches – Keener.

Ginger nut who eats double everything – Copper Pie.

It was time to tell Bee. Time to tell Bee the fantastic news.

Tribe Breakfast
at Bee's

We shouted 'thank you' a hundred times and ran back to Bee's. Jonno held Doodle's tag-less collar which made him lopsided so he got a bit left behind. Copper Pie hammered on Bee's front door. I rang the bell, even though it doesn't work. Fifty yelled through the letterbox.

Bee's mum shouted, 'I'm coming,' a bit crossly, and opened the door just as Jonno caught up with us. He let go of the collar and Doodle flew through the door. I can't properly describe what happened next. Bee came charging down the stairs and threw her arms round Doodle and there were tears all down her face and all down her mum's. Jonno pressed his face into Doodle's fur. The relief was amazing. My face started to ache because of the non-stop smiling. I wasn't a dog-murderer. I was just Keener again.

Bee's mum is a wicked cook and she loves feeding people, so she started frying things and we had a Tribe breakfast of some kind of omelette followed by hot chocolate with whipped cream and almond biscuits. Doodle had treats too, dog biscuits in gravy.

I couldn't believe that I was having biscuits for breakfast for the second day running, and that so much had happened in between. But that's Tribe for you. I don't know why, but ever since we've been Tribers, life's got livelier.

Bee's Birthday

Saving Antarctica

It was Wednesday six p.m. and that meant it was the weekly Tribe meeting in the Tribehouse. Fifty was sitting on the safe, and we were all on the bench except Bee who was lecturing us about something. I wasn't listening. I was working out how I could afford to buy a mountainboard without waiting until my birthday. I wished I had a June birthday like Bee's.

TRIBERS' STAR SIGNS

Bee is Gemini. They get on with Librans. They love talking and lots of them are on telly.

Jonno is Libra. They like peace and balance, and don't like taking sides.

Copper Pie is Sagittarius, tactless and sporty.

Keener is Scorpio, a water sign. They can be obsessive.

Fifty is Pisces, another water sign. Can be dreamers. Two water signs together can almost be telepathic. (Explains the stealing thoughts phenomenon.)

I was about to ask Bee exactly when her birthday was when . . .

'Let's have a sponsored silence as well,' she said.

I had no idea what she was talking about. 'What for?' I said.

'For the charity day on Friday.' We have one every term. It's always the same.

'But we wear home clothes and bring in a pound,' I said.

Bee gave me her special withering look. 'Who says we can't do something else?' I don't disagree with Bee unless I absolutely have to, so I shut up.

'Not speak all day?' said Fifty.

'Only while we we're at school,' she said. 'It'll be fun.'

'It won't,' said Fifty. 'I can't be quiet *all* day.' He was probably right.

'OK. You can talk, but we'll be silent. You can be our . . . translator.'

'Translating what?' said Fifty.

'Sign language and . . . whatever.' Bee made a stop-fussing face.

'OK,' said Fifty.

That's often how things get decided. Bee suggests them, Bee persuades us, we agree. (Or we say nothing and she assumes we agree.)

'Right. We need sponsor forms and sponsors,' said Bee. 'Lots.'

'My dad won't sponsor us. He hates sponsored anything. He says people should give money to charity because it's the right thing to do, not because someone jumps out of a plane,' said Jonno.

'You'll join in though, won't you?' said Bee.

Jonno nodded. 'I'll get Ravi to sponsor me.' (Ravi is Jonno's friend from where he used to live.)

'Keener?'

'I'll get Mum.' Bee waited. 'And Dad . . . and Amy.'

That seemed to do the trick. Bee turned to Copper Pie. He was ready for her. 'Big Jim next door, Mum, Dad.'

'Fifty?'

'Can I get sponsors for interpreting?'

She thought for a second, moved her fringe (which is

more like a black-out blind) off her face, and said, 'Rewind. Let's just have one Tribe form. We'll each have it for a day and see how much we can get. Agreed?'

'But there's only two days till Friday,' I pointed out. Being able to count can be an advantage.

Bee paused. I grinned. Getting one over on her is rare.

'OK,' she said. 'Text any sponsors you get to Keener. He can keep the sponsor form. And can you make it too, Keener?' She smiled her just-do-as-I-say smile. 'Don't forget to include the name of the charity.'

'What is the name of the charity?' I asked.

'Twenty forty-one.' The way Bee said it made me think I should know what *twenty forty-one* was. 'Didn't you listen to *anything* in assembly?' she said, rolling her eyes. Asking how to spell it didn't seem like a good move.

'What sort of charity has a name that's all numbers?' asked Copper Pie.

'A charity for sad people who like adding up,' said Fifty.

'They're called mathematicians,' said Jonno.

'Or Keeners,' said Fifty. *Thanks!*

'Listen,' said Bee. She sliced the air with a karate chop to shut us up.

'2041 isn't the sort of thing we usually have,' said Fifty. 'We usually have donkey sanctuaries.'

'Who cares about donkeys?' said Copper Pie.

'Someone on the school council cared or it wouldn't have been picked,' I said.

BEE'S LECTURE ON 2041
(WHICH IS A DATE)

Antarctica is safe from hotels, chip shops and piles of rotting nappies because there's a deal that everyone agreed to that protects it. But in 2041 the deal ends.

So Robert Swann set up a charity to make sure that the people who will be making the decision in 2041 realise how important it is for the whole world to keep Antarctica's 5 million mile square of solid ice free and wild. He means us. It's up to kids like us to tell everyone that tourists and rich people and idiots mustn't be allowed to ruin the last bit of the world that's totally natural.

'So who on the school council cares about 2041?' asked Jonno.

No idea, I thought.

Bee looked round at us all, smirking as though she knew something we didn't.

'It can't have been you,' said Jonno. 'You're not on the council.'

'But it was chosen, wasn't it?' said Fifty.

Bee did a slow nod.

'How come?' I said.

'She bribed them,' said Copper Pie.

'With ice creams,' said Jonno.

'Glacier mints,' said Fifty, getting the joke before I did.

'Penguins,' said Copper Pie. 'The chocolate ones.'

I tried to think of an Antarctic connection too – complete blank.

'I didn't bribe anyone,' said Bee. 'I told Amir the facts and he persuaded the council. So there.'

Amir is Bee's buddy from Year 5. She's trained him so that he's even more of an eco-freak than she is.

'I've got to go,' said Copper Pie. He put out his hand ready for a Tribe handshake. We all slapped ours down on top. One, two three . . . our hands shot up in the air.

'Get lots of sponsors, everyone,' said Bee.

Silence

On Friday, the day of the sponsored silence, registration didn't go that well. The first Triber's name Miss Walsh called out was Fifty's.

'Good morning, Fifty.'

'Good morning, Miss Walsh.'

The list went on and the next Triber she got to was Jonno.

'Good morning, Jonno,' she said.

Jonno nodded. Miss Walsh didn't see so she said 'Good morning' a bit louder. Jonno nodded again, but when she looked up he'd finished. She stared at him. He nodded some more. Even though she could see him nodding, she waited for him to speak. We all knew that wasn't going to happen.

Fifty tried to answer for him. 'Jonno's —'

'Jonno can speak for himself, thank you,' said our frosty teacher. I took the Tribe sponsor form out of my pocket. If I showed her she'd understand, but not before she'd shouted at me. I put it back and left it to our interpreter.

Fifty tried again. 'Actually, he —'

'What part of "Jonno can speak for himself" did you not understand?' Miss Walsh retied her twisty bun. She does that when she's cross. Someone needed to explain, and quickly. But only Fifty was allowed to speak. And he wasn't allowed to speak because Miss Walsh wouldn't let him.

Eventually she moved on to the next name on the register. 'An especially good morning to you, Bee.'

There was no way out of this mess. Miss Walsh stared at Bee. Bee nodded. I turned and looked at Fifty. He shrugged. Shrugging was no use. He was meant to be doing the talking. Copper Pie obviously thought the same. He reached over to Fifty's desk, yanked him out of his chair and pushed him forwards. Fifty looked down at the floor and spoke at five times normal speed.

'We're-having-a-sponsored-silence-to-raise-money-for-the-charity-with-all-the-numbers-and-I-can-speak-but-the-other-Tribers-can't-so-they-can't-say-"Good-morning".' He looked up. 'Sorry.'

Miss Walsh put her head in her hands for a second – I think she was taking a few deep breaths – and carried on without bothering to say my name or Copper Pie's. At the end she shut the register and said, 'Charity day is an important day each term when we think about helping others. It would have helped me if the children involved in the sponsored silence had informed me rather than arriving at school already mute. And as the silence is taking place in school time, it should be agreed with the school.' She turned to look at Fifty. 'I'd like you, as the token talker, to go to the Head's office and ask permission for the sponsored silence to take place.' Miss Walsh is no fun.

Fifty stood up and headed for the door. Since we stopped being Keener, Bee, Fifty, Copper Pie and Jonno and became Tribe we'd been in trouble for loads of stuff, mostly not our fault. I thought about the other times we'd been sent to the Head.

PERFECTLY REASONABLE THINGS THE TRIBERS HAVE DONE
(and had to explain to the Head)

- We took over assembly to save an endangered stag beetle. It was about to be pulverised by a bulldozer to make way for a herb garden.
- We recruited some younger kids to work as slaves filling one thousand water bombs for the summer fair. What's wrong with that? We paid them.

> • We were caught teasing Marco about his lunch. But we weren't teasing, we were just being nosy.
> • We uncovered a thief, but not everyone liked the way we ran our investigation.

The list would have been longer but Fifty came back. 'The Head said "a Tribe that is silent would be a welcome change from a Tribe that makes more than its share of noise".' He smiled at Miss Walsh. 'She sponsored us five pounds if we go all day without a squeak.'

Miss Walsh looked like she wanted to go home and cry on her pillow. I don't think she should be a teacher. She should be a Samaritan who answers the phone to people who are upset or someone who stuffs red shiny hearts into the teddies at the Build-a-Bear Workshop.

Fifty sat down. Miss Walsh told us to get out our maths books.

'OK, class. As you know, we're spending the last half term of Year 6 going over the topics we've covered this year, so today it's perimeters and areas.' There was groaning. 'We're going to calculate the areas and perimeters of five things in the room, being careful to use the appropriate units.'

Alice's hand shot up, as usual.

Miss Walsh sighed. 'What is it, Alice?'

'Can I measure the door?'

'Yes, Alice.'

'Can I do the bin?' shouted out Jamie. Jamie has never learnt to put his hand up. He just shouts out.

'No, you can't,' said Miss Walsh.

'That's not fair. If she can do the door, why can't I do the bin?'

Miss Walsh spoke through gritted teeth. 'You can't do the bin because we haven't learnt the formula for calculating the area of circles. We've done squares and rectangles and they've all had straight edges and right angles.'

'Can I do the window?' shouted Jamie. You could tell Miss Walsh had given up because she said 'All right' without even looking at him.

There were a few more minutes of instructions, like 'record all the dimensions' and 'draw a sketch before you do the sum', and finally we were ready to pick our five objects. I chose things I could reach without getting up. Callum, also known as the evil Hog, decided to irritate me by measuring my desk, which is the same size as his.

He whispered, 'If you say nothing it means you wet the bed.' I ignored him. He moved over to Bee's desk and tried the same thing. She stamped on his foot. Miss Walsh saw.

'Why did you do that, Bee?'

Bee picked up her pencil and wrote something on her maths book.

'Didn't,' said Callum.

Didn't what? I thought. Bee held up her book and

shoved the writing towards Callum's face, which meant I could see it too.

He tried to make me talk to stop me raising
money to save the PLANET.

'Callum, why don't you find something to measure *away* from Bee?' said Miss Walsh.

'OK.' Callum picked up his book and went over to where Jonno was measuring the whiteboard. He whispered something. Jonno picked up the whiteboard rubber and turned round to face Callum. He smiled, and started to rub Callum out, starting with his face. He didn't actually touch him, he just mimed rubbing out as though Callum was a drawing we didn't need any more. Callum stormed off to measure the window with his only friend, Jamie.

Callum was determined to spoil the sponsored silence, but it would take more than him to trip up Tribe. If we say we're doing something, we're doing it.

Happy
Birthday

At break we hung around on our patch under the trees, apart from Copper Pie who was kicking a football against the wall. Jonno studied the tree stump – he's always on the lookout for weevils. Bee stared at the rest of the kids mucking about in the playground while Fifty talked to himself. I got the sponsor form out to convince myself that a day of zipped-up mouths was worth the effort. Including the Head's contribution we'd got forty-three pounds.

Lily came over and brought out a present from behind her back. 'Happy Birthday, Bee.' It was about the size of an apple, wrapped in silver paper.

I almost spoke, but stopped myself just in time. *Why hadn't Bee reminded us it was her birthday?*

Bee mouthed 'Thank you' and took the silver apple.

Jonno stood up and made a no-one-mentioned-a-birth-day face. (I realised that someone else had remembered – Miss Walsh gave Bee a special 'Good morning' but I was too busy being silent to notice.) Inside the silver paper was a lime-green rubber ball with a hole with jagged edges attached to a keyring. Bee held it up and made what-is-it? signs.

Lily laughed. 'It's for storing your dog-poo bags when you take Doodle for a walk. And it's Fairtrade.' Bee laughed, but without the sound, and clipped the keyring on to her watch-strap and gave Lily a thumbs up. Lily went back to the world where people actually speak, leaving us back in the world of nothing. We had a conversation about Bee's birthday by writing messages on our phones. After loads of tapping it turned out that Bee hadn't mentioned her birthday because she wasn't having a party, and she wasn't having a party because her parents couldn't afford go-karting or laser quest or whatever. Jonno suggested she had a tea party. Bee thought for a bit, then asked if he meant it, and we all wrote *yes*. So Fifty got the job of calling Bee's mum and asking if we could all come over for a last-minute birthday tea.

'OK,' said Fifty after he ended the call. 'Bee's mum and dad are going to the opening of some new Italian restaurant at seven-thirty but her brothers will come over and look after us – not that we need babysitting!' Fifty grinned. 'We can watch a film afterwards.' There was clapping. Fifty carried on.

'And Bee's mum said,' (out came his Italian accent) '"Thank you for persuading Beatrice to celebrate her birthday".'

Bee stuck her tongue out. She doesn't like being teased about her Italian family.

'And she said to invite Lily, as well as all the Tribers.'

The four of us trooped over to where Copper Pie was kicking the ball repeatedly against the same spot on the wall, like a machine. Fifty filled him in. He grinned and stuck out his fist for the fist of friendship. Fifty went off to tell Lily. All we had left to do was text our mums we wouldn't be in for tea.

The day had got a whole lot better. We couldn't talk all day at school but we'd be together all evening. Birthdays are good, even other people's.

A
Rich Stranger

In history, not being allowed to speak was a bonus. Miss Walsh fired questions at everyone while I daydreamed that I got a massive cheque through the post from a stranger that I once helped (not that I've ever helped a stranger).

TRIBERS' DAYDREAMS

COPPER PIE: Includes these words, in any order: football, win, score, hero.

FIFTY: Lead role in a play where he gets to dress up in old-fashioned clothes, like a Tudor or something, and sing.

BEE: Serious reporter on location in the Gobi desert talking about some eco-success like

> saving the last remaining Bactrians (two-humped camels).
>
> KEENER: 'In this clip Keener executes the most high-performance manoeuvre possible on a surfboard: a rodeo flip.'
>
> JONNO: A big family meal with all of his brothers and sisters, maybe seven or eight, and noise and chips and bad manners.

I didn't take any notice of what was going on until Copper Pie stood up, picked a few things up off the floor by his chair, walked over to Callum and sprinkled them over his head.

'What on earth!' spluttered Miss Walsh. Copper Pie pointed at Callum, did a throwing action and slapped himself on the back of the head. He did it three times with his face going more like the colour of his hair every time. He was really angry (but quite funny to watch). Luckily Fifty had got the hang of translating. He stood up and defended Copper Pie like a barrister stating the case in front of a judge.

'I believe Copper Pie to have been hit on the back of the head by various missiles.' Fifty bent down to study the evidence. 'Including rubbers, screwed-up paper and what looks like extra-large bogeys, thrown by Callum.'

'Sit down, Fifty,' said Miss Walsh. 'Is this true, Callum?'

'No. I didn't throw anything.'

Copper Pie leant over Callum's desk and did a cutthroat

sign. Callum pushed him away. It was all getting a bit stressy. I was pleased I couldn't talk – it took away any responsibility to help. I looked at Miss Walsh to see what she was going to do. Nothing much, it seemed. Jonno leant over and tapped Copper Pie on the back. It meant, 'He's not worth the bother.' Copper Pie sat back down.

Miss Walsh is useless at sorting out trouble. She writes the names of whoever's involved in the sad-face column on the board and threatens that if they end up there twice more, they'll see the Head. It doesn't matter who's right and who's wrong. She says, 'Three strikes and you're out', as if she's an American baseball coach.

THREE STRIKES AND YOU'RE OUT

In baseball if you miss the ball three times, you're out – it's called a strikeout. 24 of the 51 American states decided to use that rule to deal with criminals. It's called the Three Strikes Law. If someone is convicted three times for any offence, whether it's shoplifting or murder, they get sent to prison. (Or in Miss Walsh's case, sent out.)

Callum's name went on the board, followed by Copper Pie's. And then it was lunch.

The dinner ladies didn't like us pointing so Fifty asked for our food. We sat at our favourite table in the corner. Fifty talked a bit, but getting no answers was boring so he went and sat on Ed's table. We could hear them laughing while we sat in silence.

I slept with my eyes open all afternoon. Dull wasn't the word, it was mind-numbing. The clock hands crawled round as though time had its brakes on. The only thing that kept me awake was the occasional bit of debris hitting the back of my head. I knew who was doing it, but I didn't complain because I knew I'd end up in the sad-face column.

Two minutes before the bell, the Head came to see how we were doing. That's what she said anyway. But I think, like Callum, she just wanted to enjoy the fact we couldn't speak.

As soon as we were out of the playground, I said, 'Remind me never to agree to a sponsored silence again.'

'Same,' said Fifty.

When I got home there was an empty cement bag on the table. On closer inspection I realised it was a cement bag that had been turned into a different kind of bag. Mum had been extra efficient.

'Do you like it?' she said.

'Not much,' I said. 'But Bee will.'

'As soon as I got your text about the party I knew where to go for a present. I was going to buy a recycled glass bracelet but I figured she might prefer the bag.'

'You figured right. Thanks.'

I went to the cupboard to get some wrapping paper and a card from the stockpile. I chose one with a cupcake on it, scribbled inside and taped it to the pressie. I was ready. There was time for a lie down in my hammock. I swayed from side to side and thought about all the parties we'd been to.

TRIBERS' FUNNIEST PARTIES

- Animal party. Copper Pie was a meat-eating dinosaur and tried to eat the other animals.
- Soft play. Someone was sick in the ball pit.
- Harry Potter party. Copper Pie was Ron. Keener was a broomstick.
- Bee's recycling party. We made treasure boxes in her garden from junk.
- Flo's games party. She ran away with the middle of the pass-the-parcel.
- Fifty's go-karting party. He was too small so he had to watch.

'Are you going to wear a shirt?' Mum shouted up the stairs.

'No need. It's only tea,' I shouted back. Every Christmas she buys me a stripy shirt, like a deckchair, that I have to wear to family dos. But I will *never* wear one in front of my friends. I was wearing my favourite Saltrock T-shirt – perfect for tuna with beans (Bee's mum's speciality) and a chocolate pudding. Or whatever we were having.

Top
Tea

Fifty and Jonno were already sitting at the kitchen table drinking Coke when I pushed open the red door to Bee's kitchen. I said, 'Happy Birthday' and gave Bee the present. She really liked it. Only Bee could get excited about a re-used cement bag with a red strap. I didn't want a Coke so I had orange juice. There was a checked cloth on the table and candles and eight places. Lily came next, then Copper Pie, then Bee's dad, and then the twins. Bee's brothers are old – university age, except they don't go to university. They lived at Bee's until Bee's dad threw them out because they were too old to live at home. They live with a really cool actress now. I have no idea whether they have jobs, and I only know one of their names – Patrick. I hoped someone might say the name of the other one, because it's embarrassing not knowing the name of one of your best friend's family.

'Louis, take the basket.' *Excellent.* The other brother's name was Louis. 'Go ahead,' said Bee's mum as Louis put the basket of garlic bread on the table. It smelt lush. I waited for someone else's hand to shoot out before I took a piece. Another basket followed. This time the bread had melted cheese on it. I stuck with the non cheese. Melted cheese is too sticky. A bowl of mushrooms came next. Bee spooned some onto her plate.

'Same,' said Fifty. He held out his plate so we all did as well. *Tasty!* There were more and more bowls and plates and baskets coming all the time. There was also loads of noise from the mini-conversations going on round the table. It was much better than tea at my house. Bee's mum and dad hovered by the cooker while we all ate. Bee's brothers were funny. They teased her – something we'd never dare do. After a while the plates all got cleared. I felt quite full but I'd kept a space for pudding. But pudding didn't come – more food came. This time it was a massive washing-up size bowl of pasta, that Bee's dad smothered in parmesan cheese from a really cool silver grater with a handle, and a pot of some sort of meat and tomato stew and, Fifty's favourite, some white beans.

'We have to go, *bambina*,' said Bee's mum. She took out her lipstick and made her lips red without looking in a mirror. 'We won't be late. Patrick, Louis, look after our guests.'

The twins lifted their glasses and both said something that sounded Italian at the same time. Bee's parents disappeared out of the kitchen door.

'Your mum should be a chef,' said Fifty. He was playing with the candles. Fire is his favourite thing, after sugar.

'She was for a while,' said Patrick. 'When we had our own restaurant.' I didn't know they used to have a restaurant. I've never known what jobs Bee's mum and dad did.

'I wouldn't mind being a baker,' said Bee. 'Making cakes and pastries.'

That started a whole long conversation that went round and round the table about things you could be, or couldn't be, or wouldn't be or might be. An Antarctic explorer, a professional football player, a newsreader, an actor, a writer, a surfer, a barrister, a bank robber, a tightrope walker.

'Funny how no one wants to work in a supermarket,' said Louis.

'I'd rather be a bin man,' said Copper Pie. 'Finished by lunchtime.'

'That's what we should do,' said Patrick. 'Life on the bins.'

'Do you work in a supermarket?' Fifty asked Louis.

'I do. And so does my brother.' Louis slapped Patrick on the back. They laughed.

'We should have stayed on at school and passed some exams,' said Patrick.

'Ignore them,' said Bee. 'They're idiots.' I didn't want to ignore them, they were interesting. I could see that Jonno

91

thought so too. (He's an only child, which he hates, and his house is quiet and tidy, which he hates, and his parents are always moving house, which he hates. He's always round at Bee's.)

'We're going to be millionaires,' said Patrick.

'As soon as we get the right idea,' said Louis.

'We're entrepreneurs,' said Patrick.

'Shelf-stacking's not for ever,' said Louis.

'We hope.' They said it together again, and laughed. They laughed almost all the time in fact. Being at Bee's in the charge of her brothers was fun, better than laser tag or a football party.

'Make way,' shouted Louis. He was carrying a tray with even more food, but this time it really was pudding. We tried to clear a space but there were too many dishes and too many people passing them in too many different directions.

Bee took over. 'Jonno, put the dirty plates by the sink. Fifty – you're on knives and forks. Copper Pie, take the pasta bowl and put it by the cooker. Keener, can you take the big pot and put it *on* the cooker? I'll put the sauce back in the fridge.' We all did as we were told. It was worth it – Louis placed a massive pavlova filled with strawberries and fluffy white cream on the table, followed by a brown and yellow custardy-looking thing. (No prizes for guessing which one I wanted.)

Patrick picked up the whole pavlova, tipped the plate

and pretended to let it slide into his mouth. Louis took it off him and started dishing out.

'Leave room for the birthday girl's birthday cake,' he said. 'The best is yet to come.'

We all groaned. Bee's mum really knows how to cook. If we lived with Bee we'd all be the size of yetis. I loaded my spoon with equal amounts of meringue, cream and strawberry, opened my mouth and scoffed. It was good. I was happy. The sponsored silence was no fun whatsoever but Bee's last-minute party was great.

But unfortunately it was all about to go wrong – big time.

Slim, Bodger, Rasher and Teapot

The back door opened.

'Hey, Slim,' said Patrick. 'Come and feast.'

Someone called Slim came in. He was skinny. 'What's happening?' he said.

'It's Bee's birthday.'

'Happy birthday, Bee,' said Slim.

Bee didn't smile. I got the feeling Slim wasn't her favourite person, or maybe she just didn't want him at her party.

The conversation slowed down, partly because pudding was delicious, and partly because Patrick stayed over by the cooker chatting to Slim, who was eating the leftover meat stew straight from the pot with a serving spoon. There was a knock on the door and it opened again.

'Hey, Bodger,' said Patrick. In came someone called

Bodger. He had hair redder than Copper Pie's and curlier than Fifty's, sticking out like a frill from under a blue and green stripy beanie.

'Any left?' said Bodger. There was nodding from Slim. They shared the serving spoon. Bee definitely wasn't smiling.

'OK, everyone,' said Louis. 'I think it's cake time.' He disappeared out of the door to the hall and came back a couple of minutes later with about fifty candles burning on top of a mound of chocolate. He started the singing.

'Buon Compleanno a te,
'Buon Compleanno a te,
'Buon Compleanno cara Beatrice,
'Buon Compleanno a te.

We all joined in, in English, except Patrick who was in a huddle with Bodger and Slim. Bee did one massive puff and blew all the candles out.

'Are you cutting the cake, Bee?' asked Louis.

'Of course.' Bee took the knife and started slicing. I didn't think I was going to fit it in but the sponge bit was like eating a sweet cloud and the chocolate bit was heaven so I managed.

We'd been sitting at the table for ages so I was quite glad when Bee got up. She offered to help clear but Louis said he'd do it. Patrick seemed to have forgotten it was Bee's birthday. We abandoned the kitchen for the comfy sofa in front of the telly. Five of us squashed on together which left Fifty to sit on the footstool.

Bee had chosen *The Italian Job* – the original version with the minis and the coach hanging over the cliff. It's a Tribe favourite.

TRIBERS' FAVOURITE FILMS

FIFTY: The Sound of Music (he knows all the words) and Bambi.

JONNO: The Great Escape, because he likes 'The Scrounger' and the blind man.

BEE: Free Willy, Hoot!, Eight Below. Anything to do with saving animals.

KEENER: Jaws, which is odd because he doesn't like blood.

COPPER PIE: Sky Sports (clearly not a film), The Tooth Fairy (a bad film).

And Lily's: The Princess Diaries (vomit).

While we were waiting for the *play movie* icon to come up, there was more knocking at the back door followed by at least one, maybe two, new voices. I looked over at Bee. She shrugged. 'It was always like this when the twins lived here. Random people arriving and leaving and eating and sleeping and leaving hoodies and taking Dad's coat and using all the loo roll. That's why Dad made them leave.'

The beginning of the film shows Michael Caine leaving prison. It's not noisy like it is later when there are car chases. We could hear Patrick and Louis and their mates shouting in the kitchen. We put up with it for a while but we couldn't really hear, or concentrate on what was happening. Bee pressed *pause* and went to sort them out. We heard her giving them the Bee treatment. It works on us. She came back and pressed *play*. It was quieter for maybe ten minutes, but then they started laughing and yelling and there was some crashing and banging like chairs falling over and pans being dropped. Bee turned up the volume, but *The Italian Job* couldn't drown out Slim and Bodger and whoever else was in Bee's kitchen. She cranked it up again. It was no good. On top of everything else we could hear singing, the sort you'd hear at a football match. Bee paused it again. The noise was deafening. It sounded like there was at least a rugby team in there. And breaking glass! *Maybe they were fighting* . . .

'I'll come with you,' said Jonno. 'If that will help.'

'Thanks,' said Bee, 'but they probably won't take any notice. My brothers wouldn't manage to behave properly even if someone like the Queen was here.' It wasn't like Bee to give in. I felt really bad for her. I mean, it was her birthday and her brothers were ruining the film, ruining the whole evening.

'Come on, let's go and talk to them,' said Jonno. 'It's worth a try.'

Copper Pie got up and marched straight into the kitchen without waiting for anyone else. 'Shut up!' I heard him shout as I walked into the hall. 'We're trying to watch a film and all we can hear is you lot.'

For a moment there was complete and utter silence. It was almost funny. Like everyone had been waxworked.

'Sorry,' said a stranger who was helping himself to Bee's birthday cake.

'Maybe leave some cake, Rasher,' said Louis. The stranger looked up at Bee and put what was left of the huge lump of cake in his hand back on the plate.

'We were just chatting, Bee. We'll be off out soon.' Patrick gave Bee a cheesy smile. Bee didn't smile back.

'Don't be a bore,' said the fourth friend – who was posh. 'It's Friday night. And that's the weekend. Yay!'

Louis tapped him on the shoulder. 'Teapot, my sister's not finding this funny and you're not helping.' (I know we've got odd nicknames but Slim, Bodger, Rasher and Teapot are totally stupid.)

'Why don't you leave now,' said Bee. 'We'll be fine without you.'

'But we're babysitting,' said Louis. 'Mum said.'

'You're hardly looking after me, are you?' There were tears in Bee's eyes.

'Time to go, everyone,' said Louis. 'Patrick, you go with the others and I'll wait for Mum.'

'Come with us. Bee'll be fine, won't you?' said Patrick.

'We can't leave her. She's *eleven*,' said Louis. He waved his arm across the room. 'They're all *eleven*.' Patrick didn't look as if he cared whether we were eleven, or whether we were elves. He just wanted to go out. I decided the brothers (well him anyway) weren't as nice as I thought.

Bodger, Slim and Rasher headed for the door.

'Sorry,' said Slim. 'Just having a laugh.'

Teapot stayed where he was — leaning back on his chair with one foot resting on the edge of the table. Copper Pie kicked Teapot's leg away and he nearly fell over backwards. 'Steady on,' he said. (I thought people only spoke like that in old films.) Then he got up and left.

Louis followed them all out. 'I'll be back in a sec, Bee.'

The back door banged shut. *Phew! Crisis over.* The exact second I had that thought there were two quick hard knocks on the front door. *Or maybe not . . .*

Knock,
Knock . . .

We all looked at each other. There were two more short sharp raps on the door. We did more looking.

'It must be them,' said Lily. 'Mucking about.'

'Must be,' said Jonno.

'Same,' said Fifty.

'So no point answering,' said Copper Pie.

'Unless it's your mum,' I said to Bee.

'She has a *key*, Keener.'

Whoever was knocking definitely didn't have a key. This time there were three raps.

'I'd better get it,' said Bee. 'Maybe Patrick's stuffed Louis in a tree or something.' *Not the first explanation I'd have thought of, but Bee knows her brothers better than we do.*

Bee hurried to the door and we shadowed her. I don't

know why but I was a bit spooked. She opened the door.

'You took your time —' The person at the door stopped mid-sentence. *Oh dear!* It was Sergeant Farrow, dog-finder, little-sister-finder, and, at this moment, not the nice police-man we knew, but an angry-looking policeman. He had the same woman officer with him.

'Hello,' said Fifty.

'Not you kids again,' he said. *Not pleased to see us* was an understatement.

'Is there a problem?' said Jonno.

'Yes, that is usually why we bang on doors at . . .' He looked at his watch. '. . . ten o'clock at night.'

What had we done? The only thing I could think was that maybe *The Italian Job* was a 15 certificate and the TV licensing people had a monitor inside the telly and could see we were only eleven.

'Are your parents in?' said the woman police officer.

Bee shook her head. 'But my brother's here.'

'Where exactly?' said Sergeant Farrow.

'In the garden, I think,' said Bee.

He scanned our faces before he continued. 'There's been a complaint about the noise coming from this house. And suggestions of a fight.' I knew he thought it was us. If only Bodger and Teapot and that lot hadn't just left.

'Sorry,' said Jonno. 'It wasn't us.'

'Of course it wasn't,' said Sergeant Farrow. 'It was all the other people in the house.' He made a point of looking behind us for all the non-existent people. 'Shall we see if we can find that brother?'

We moved aside to let the two of them in. Bee went to the kitchen, they followed and we trailed behind. No whispering, no funny looks. I don't know about the others but I was thinking about the Three Strikes Law – we'd lost the dog, stolen Probably Rose and were guilty of being in a noisy house. Did that mean we were in big young-offenders'-institute-type trouble?

Louis came in the back door at the same time as Bee stepped into the kitchen from the hall. He saw the uniforms. They saw him.

'Well, well, another familiar face,' said Sergeant Farrow.

Louis went beetroot, worse than the raspberry colour I go. 'What's up?' he said.

'The same thing I was called here for a few months ago as I remember – a disturbance, reported by your neighbour.'

'It's all over,' said Louis. 'It was just some friends.'

'Like last time. A few high spirits, was it?'

'That's right.' Louis's face darkened to maroon. 'Sorry.'

'So you probably think we should just let it go, do you?'

'We'd be very grateful,' said Bee. 'It's my birthday.' As she said *birthday* her face crumpled up. It hadn't exactly been a brilliant day.

'Well, I'm afraid that's not quite how it works. Let's take some names and addresses, shall we?' My heart accelerated to maximum speed ready to burst out and run away up the street on its own.

The woman police officer got out a pad and asked who lived at the address. Only Bee answered. When Louis explained that he didn't live there any more things got worse.

'I think I'd better make a call. Is there a number I can get your parents on, Bee?'

Bee hesitated, but she had no choice. She told him her dad's mobile number. The police sent the Tribers (plus Lily) to sit in the living room. We waited in complete silence – not a sponsored one, a scared one.

Over
and Out

Bee's mum and dad came home in a taxi. We heard the brakes, the car doors open and slam, Bee's dad pay the taxi driver and the key in the door. It made me realise that with the volume up so high the neighbours probably heard as much of *The Italian Job* as we did, as well as the banging, crashing and breaking glass. *What was the breaking glass?*

The footsteps went from the front door along the hall to the kitchen. And then there was shouting. It was Bee's mum. And she was livid. It was half Italian, half English so I got the idea, but not the detail. That was probably good. I really wanted to go home. None of us were talking. And the delicious tea seemed like it happened days ago.

There was another knock on the door. We all sat up a bit taller, like mongooses on high alert. I heard a voice that sounded familiar – it was Copper Pie's dad.

'Bee's mum must have rung our parents,' whispered Fifty.

Copper Pie's dad came straight into the living room. 'Time to go home,' he said.

'Bye,' shouted C.P. His dad nudged him. 'Thank you, Bee.'

My dad came next. Our departure wasn't quite so quick. Dad did a diversion via the kitchen to talk to Sergeant Farrow. 'Good evening,' said Dad.

I stood behind him, stared at the floor and tried to work out how many tiles there were altogether. Louis must have told them all that it wasn't the Tribers who were to blame, which was a relief. Dad spent a few minutes murmuring stuff that was meant to help the situation, and then he said the magic words, 'We'll be off, then.'

Absolutely, I thought. I said, 'Thank you for the lovely tea' to Bee's mum and we scarpered. Well, I did. Dad walked normally. I was in such a hurry to get out I didn't even say goodbye to the Tribers.

Saturday

I woke up, pleased to be in my own bed knowing I could talk all day if I liked, or not speak at all, and, assuming no one lost a dog, or a sister, or had a noisy party, I could avoid any more run-ins with the police. But my next thought was about Bee. About how she had a rubbish party. The thought didn't last long — it wasn't my fault, it was her brothers'. I was soon daydreaming about freshly waxed boards riding massive waves that went on forever. My phone rang — it was Jonno.

'Keener, I've been thinking about Bee. She didn't have a very good birthday, so I thought we could try again. I thought we could have a surprise Tribe party in the Tribehouse.' I was about to answer but he carried on. 'I've called Fifty — he's cool. So's Copper Pie.'

'And so am I,' I said.

'Good. So, we're meeting at the Tribehouse at twelve o'clock. Ask your mum to donate something for the party. My dad's given me a piñata. It's a star. He brought it back from Mexico. It's real. See you later.' He'd gone. I lay there wondering what a 'real' piñata was.

Eventually I smelt bacon – that meant Dad had started breakfast duty. It's his Saturday job. I get brought a bacon sarnie that I eat in front of the computer before it's time to go to my swimming lesson. Amy has French toast with Marmite in bed. Flo has fried egg and potato waffles in front of the telly before she goes to ballet. Mum has tea, a big pot, in bed with the magazine from the paper. Dad has bacon, egg and beans and reads the other bits of the paper. We always set off late and get there just in time, thanks to nifty short cuts.

At the pool I remembered I was meant to be bringing something for the party. I asked Dad to call Mum and ask her if she could find some party snacks and drinks for me to pick up later. 'Will do,' said Dad. 'After I've dropped Flo.' Dad goes for a large cappuccino while I'm doing 30-second lengths and Flo's messing about in a tutu.

I checked every single locker before and after swimming, looking for forgotten pounds to put towards my mountain-board fund. It was one of my worst mornings – only one measly pound coin. My best is eight.

Dad dropped me at Fifty's early. The Tribehouse was

empty so I went up to the house.

'Hello, Keener,' shouted Fifty's mum – the radio was on quite loud. She turned it down. I think she'd been dancing because she was panting.

'Is Fifty here?' I asked.

'No, but he will be soon. He's gone to get me the paper. His dad's got a wedding today,' (Fifty's dad has two jobs – he does wedding photographs as well as being a postman) 'and Rose is asleep so I'm stranded.' She smiled. She's always nice. 'Come and sit down.' I sat on a stool. My legs dangled.

'Did Fifty tell you about the party?' I asked.

'He did. And I think it's an excellent way to make up for yesterday's disappointment. In fact, I've got an idea. Let's decorate the hut.'

Whether I thought it was a good idea or not wouldn't have mattered. Fifty's mum was off. She got on her knees and all sorts of stuff came flying out of her cupboards. She bundled it all up, told me to get the Blu-Tack and the Sellotape, grabbed the baby monitor and off we went down the garden.

'Find the other end of the bunting, will you, Keener?' I gave her a blank look. She pointed at the triangular flags on a string. It took a while to untangle them but by the time Fifty came through the Tribe flap we'd wound a line of flags all the way round the hut and were on to the tinsel.

'That's for Christmas, Mum,' said Fifty.

'There are no rules, Fifty.' She tossed him some. 'Hang it from the string.' He did. It looked like there were shiny caterpillars crawling down the walls. Bee was going to love it.

'Can we pick some of them?' I asked, pointing to a load of flowers growing at the bottom of the garden (which is like a wilderness).

'Poppies? Yes, why not. Let's bunch them up and hang them from the bunting too.' Some grizzling came from the baby monitor. Fifty's mum was having too much fun to bother with Rose. 'Get your sister for me, darling.'

Fifty went off to get his favourite person in the whole world. We did the poppies. I got a text from Bee, but I didn't know what to tell her so I ignored it.

'That's brilliant,' said a mass of fluffy hair. It was Jonno, wriggling awkwardly through the flap. He was holding the piñata and a plate. 'Take this, Keener.' I relieved him of the plate. It was food – little pastry-looking things.

'That looks nice,' said Fifty's mum.

'Dad did it,' said Jonno. 'And he gave me this piñata.' Jonno held up an orange star-shape. 'It's a proper one from Mexico, made of clay, but there's nothing in it, and I haven't got a stick.'

'We need to fill it up then,' said Fifty's mum.

'Dad said they used to fill them with nuts and fruit,' said Jonno.

'Good idea,' she said.

'No way,' said Fifty, coming down the garden holding

Rose. 'It's a party. We need sweets.'

'Yes,' said Rose. She's just like her brother – sugar-mad. It's because in their house everything's organic and chewy and made from brown rice.

'I could bring some over later,' I said. 'What time is the party?'

'I don't know,' said Jonno. 'I haven't invited Bee yet. She texted me earlier but I wasn't sure what to tell her.'

'Same,' said Fifty. 'You can't invite someone to their own surprise.'

Rose stuck two fingers up Fifty's nose.

'Don't do that, Rose. You're all sticky.' Fifty put her down on the grass. She stood there for a few seconds and then flopped back onto her fat nappy. She put her arms up – that means *pick me up*. They only reached the top of her head. I'd hate to have arms that short.

'We don't have to invite her. We'll just tell her we're meeting here.'

'OK. What time?'

'You said twelve o'clock,' said the redhead, wriggling awkwardly through the Tribe flap. It was Copper Pie, holding two plastic bags and a Quality Street tin.

'What time *tonight*,' said Jonno. 'Not now.'

'Take the tin,' said Copper Pie. Inside there was a chocolate cake with roses made of white chocolate on the top and *Bee* written in dark chocolate.

'Your mum never did that,' I said. Copper Pie's mum is

absolutely not the sort of person to spend hours decorating a cake.

'Same,' said Fifty.

'She did. She said the least she could do was make an effort for Bee as her party was busted by the cops.' Copper Pie grinned as he said that – I think he liked the idea that we were *busted*.

'What's in the bags?' asked Jonno.

'Party stuff from the nursery.' Copper Pie dumped one bag down. 'And junk food.' Down went the other one. Copper Pie's mum had sent him round with plastic cups, plates, bowls, straws, candles for the cake, party poppers, serviettes and balloons. There were also crisps, two packs of biscuits (party rings and wafers), a bottle of blackcurrant squash and two packs of mini-pork pies (C.P.'s favourites).

We blew up the balloons and tied them round the door. Fifty's mum fetched a rug to put on the Tribehouse floor, but when we laid everything out on it there was no room for bodies. We brought the rug back outside, picnic-style. Keeping Rose away from the biscuits was tricky so Fifty's mum took her up to the house for lunch. I was pretty hungry too.

'We still haven't decided what time,' I said.

'What about five o'clock?' said Fifty.

We all said 'OK,' at the same time. Five o'clock it was. I disappeared off home for lunch, and to see what Mum had got for me to bring to the party. It was going to be good.

Better
and Better

It was getting better and better. At lunch (sausages in baguettes) Dad said, 'I could fix a net to the ceiling of the Tribehouse and fill it with helium balloons, if you like?' *Absolutely, I like!* He did that for Flo's birthday.

'Thanks,' I said.

'Is there some helium left?' asked Mum.

'We've got enough for a dozen balloons or so, I should think.' Dad winked at me. Mum has no idea what Dad buys on the internet. There are three canisters of helium in the cupboard in the attic – it's Dad's private store.

Mum had made a plate of sandwiches for the party, with all my favourite fillings. She'd cut them into shapes like she did when we were little. She'd also made strawberry jelly and sprinkled hundreds and thousands over it.

TRIBERS' BEST AND WORSE SANDWICHES		
	BEST	WORST
KEENER:	Bacon	Banana & Yoghurt with Tomato Sauce
BEE:	Brie & Rocket	Processed Cheese Slices in White Plastic Bread
COPPER PIE:	Meat & Pickle	A no-meat, no-pickle salad sandwich
JONNO:	Hoisin Duck wrap	Marmite
FIFTY:	Jam, Honey, Chocolate Spread	Houmus on spelt bread

'What time's the party?' asked Dad.

'Five o'clock.'

'So if I come with you at four that should give us time to set up,' said Dad. I texted Fifty to say we were coming over early. He texted back: *don't forget sweets for pinata.*

I raided the treat box – sorted.

Almost
Five O'Clock

While I'd been at home, lots had happened at Fifty's. There was country-dancing-type music playing in the garden (quite loud – I hoped Sergeant Farrow wasn't doing his rounds), cushions round the rug for seating, and Fifty's mum was *still* decorating. The Tribehouse had a blown-up and photocopied photo of Bee with Doodle on the door, a *Happy Birthday* banner along the side, and apples and oranges all along the ridge where the roof joins the walls. It looked made-up, like a gingerbread house, which reminded me of the Gingerbread Man story that Dad used to tell Flo when she sat on his shoulders.

Dad used the staple gun to attach the balloon net while I began the balloon filling. It's boring so I did about five and then let Fifty have a go. When Jonno arrived he took

THINGS WRONG WITH 'THE GINGERBREAD MAN'

- If someone heard a cookie shouting 'Let me out. Let me out,' from inside the oven, they wouldn't let it out, they'd faint, or call the BBC and get famous for baking a talking biscuit.
- A gingerbread man would be no match for a cow or a horse or a pig or whatever else chased it. And it would get soggy as it ran in the wet grass and lose its feet, then its knees, etc.
- The fox wouldn't carry the Gingerbread Man all the way across the river, it would dunk him straightaway and eat him soggy.

over and Fifty filled the piñata with the goodies I'd collected. Dad hung it up from a branch. Copper Pie came last. By ten to five we were all ready and waiting – four Tribers, my dad, Fifty's mum and Rose.

'I'll just wait and see her face when she realises it's her party all over again,' said Dad.

'What shall we do when she comes?' said Fifty.

'Say *Happy Birthday*,' said Jonno.

'Say *Surprise!*' said Fifty's mum.

'Hide in the Tribehouse and shout *Boo!* when she opens

the door.' That was my suggestion.

'But she'll see the decorations,' said Jonno.

'And the rug,' said Dad.

'And the grub,' said Copper Pie.

'Same,' said Fifty. He looked at his watch. 'She's late.'

I looked at Jonno. 'You told her five o'clock, didn't you?'

Jonno looked behind him as though I was talking to someone standing on his heels. He looked back at me. 'I didn't tell Bee anything,' he said. 'I thought you . . .' He didn't bother finishing the sentence. He hadn't told her. And he could tell from my face that I hadn't either, and so could everyone else. *Just great!*

'Who's going to call her?' said Jonno.

'I will,' said Fifty. He held his phone to his ear for a while. 'No answer.'

'Try again,' said Copper Pie. He tried again. I tried too.

'Try her home phone,' said Fifty's mum. We waited in complete silence.

'Hello, it's Fifty. Is Bee there?' There was a pause. I assumed whoever had answered the phone had gone to get Bee.

'Oh, right. I understand. Yes. Sorry.' We all stared at Fifty waiting to hear what *Oh, right, I understand, Yes, Sorry,* meant.

'Bee's in her room,' he said. He looked worried. 'She told her mum that she texted all of us and no one texted back so she doesn't want to see us.'

Fifty's face looked how I felt. Bee first party was ruined,

and now she thought we were all ignoring her, so she was missing her surprise party. *If only I'd answered her text*, I thought. I bet I wasn't the only one thinking that.

'Ring her back,' said Fifty's mum. 'Explain what happened. Tell her about the surprise if you have to.'

'You do it, Jonno,' said Fifty.

'OK.' Jonno got his phone out. He walked down the garden into the wilderness bit. We all wanted to hear but he obviously didn't want us to listen. I didn't blame him. I'm useless on the phone – although not as bad as Copper Pie who doesn't seem to know when it's his turn to talk. Jonno turned back round to face us almost straight away.

'She won't speak to me,' he said. 'Bee's mum says she won't open her bedroom door.'

It was a crisis. We'd tried to make things better but, because me and Jonno had got confused about who was telling her, we'd made things worse.

'What shall we do?' Fifty asked his mum.

'Shall I have a word with Bee's mum?' We all nodded. Even Dad. 'Back in a tick,' she said. She scooped up Rose, marched up the garden and disappeared into the kitchen. We all waited. The Tribehouse looked like it was waiting too. And if she didn't come, the fruit would rot and the flowers would droop and the rain would wash away the photo and the tinsel would lose its shine and its fringy bits and the flags would fade. It would be like Cinderella at midnight, just ordinary again.

I sat on the ground with my head on my knees.

A Party Without
The Guest Of Honour

Nothing happened for ages. No one spoke. Fifty's mum didn't reappear. Bee didn't appear. There was no lightning or thunder, no eclipse of the sun, no meteor, no rainbow, no mass migrations of geese or invasion of flying ants. I decided to hold my breath for a while. *Maybe if I could hold it in long enough something would happen*, I thought. That was a dangerous thought because I used to hold my breath when I was younger and end up going blue and fainting. I didn't do it on purpose – it just happened when I was scared or had a shock. Amy said I did it to get my own way but that wasn't true. Anyway, I had a go ... but I didn't last long. I didn't seem to be able to stop my body from taking a breath – it did it on its own. I tried a few times but I kept taking a breath without meaning to.

'What are you doing?' said Fifty eventually. Trying not to breathe didn't seem like a good answer so I gave him my best blank look.

'You keep gasping,' said Copper Pie.

'Can't you breathe properly?' said Dad.

'I'm fine,' I said. *Time to stop the breath-holding attempts.*

'Do you think she'll come?' said Jonno.

I don't know, I thought. *But I hope so.*

'Don't know,' said Copper Pie.

'Hope so,' said Fifty. They were stealing my thoughts again.

'We should do what your mum says,' said Jonno, looking at Fifty. 'The visualising thing.' It's one of Fifty's mum's tricks to help people give up smoking, or be happier, or get thinner. It's her job.

'OK. Let's do it,' he said.

Dad looked completely confused so Fifty explained.

FIFTY'S MUM'S
VISUALISING THING

The basic idea is that if you make a picture of what you want to happen in your head, you're more likely to achieve it. It's meant to work for job interviews or passing your driving test, things like that. If you can see yourself doing it you're already training your brain to do it in real life. You have to close your eyes and forget everything else except the thing you want to visualise.

So, let's try visualising . . . learning a difficult piece on the piano. You imagine walking up to the piano, sitting on the stool and finding the piece of music. You picture yourself playing the tune perfectly, hearing it in your head, maybe seeing the audience wowed by your performance. When it's over, you stand up and close the lid before walking away. That's really important – you have to start before the event and finish after it so you know how it feels before and after.

The only trouble is, it can't make Bee come – it can only affect you, not other people you put in the picture with you. Sorry.

'Let's do it anyway,' said Dad. 'It's better than waiting. And I'd like to have a go. I might introduce visualisation into our monthly sales meetings. Get everyone imagining the biggest deal ever.'

'Just don't tell Mum,' I said. 'She thinks it's barmy.' As soon as I said that I realised I shouldn't have. I didn't mean to blurt out what Mum thinks about Fifty's mum's flower potions and all the other therapies she uses. My mum likes

Fifty's mum, but she's a doctor and doctors don't believe in rose-flavour treatments or visualising. They think it's witchcraft.

Dad saved me. 'Your mum thinks a lot of things are barmy, including me. But remember, she doesn't understand everything – she can't catch a wave, can she?' Everyone laughed, even Fifty. My mum on a surfboard wasn't something you could easily visualise.

'Come on, then,' said Jonno.

'OK. Everyone shut your eyes,' said Dad. I shut my eyes and lay back on the grass. 'Imagine you're in Fifty's garden, waiting for Bee.'

'But we are,' said Copper Pie.

'Shut up,' said Fifty. 'You have to go along with it.'

Copper Pie shut up.

Dad carried on. 'It's warm and sunny, and you're waiting for Bee to come to her surprise party. Picture the garden. The food's ready, and there are drinks and a cake. Picture the food. Picture the cake. Picture the —'

Fifty interrupted. 'Shall I take over?' Dad was obviously no good.

'OK. I'll listen and learn.'

'Get comfortable everyone.'

I already was, sun on my face, eyelids as heavy as if a hot water bottle was pressing on them. Fifty started off using a quiet, dreamy voice. He didn't tell us to picture anything, or if he did, I didn't notice. He took us all the way through from wondering whether Bee would come, to hearing a rustle by the Tribe flap, to her happy face when she saw the decorated hut. We ate the food and drank blackcurrant. It was time for the cake. '*Happy Birthday to you.*' We bashed the piñata and scrambled about for the sweets. It was like a really nice dream . . .

Wake Up, Keener

Something touched my face. I sat up really quickly and opened my eyes. The sun was far too bright. I closed my lids and made two small slits so I could focus. Fifty's face was a millimetre from mine. And he was laughing. And so were other people. I wiped my mouth. My chin was wet. I knew what that meant – I'd been dribbling in my sleep. *Great! More teasing.*

'Wakey, wakey,' said Fifty.

'You're just in time,' said Dad. *Just in time for what?* The last thing I remembered was chasing round the garden to get the sweets from the piñata.

'They should be here any second,' said Fifty's mum from behind me somewhere. *Who should be here any second?* I had lots of questions but I didn't want to ask them because I

123

knew I'd sound even more stupid than I felt.

'Keener, night, night,' said Probably Rose.

'Clever girl,' said Fifty.

'Isn't she?' said Fifty's mum, smiling at Rose.

'Her talking's really coming on,' said Dad. I was grateful for the chat about Rose. I needed to work out what was real and what was dream, and fast. I glanced up at the Tribehouse – the star piñata was still hanging, un-whacked. That was a clue. I scanned the bodies: Fifty, Fifty's mum, Probably Rose, my dad, Copper Pie, Jonno. There was still no Bee. Another clue.

'Mum, what time was it when you said they were on their way?' Fifty asked. My ears pricked up. Another clue – but who were *they*? Bee wasn't *they*. Bee was *she*. I worked it out quite quickly considering the clever half of my brain was still somewhere else – someone was bringing Bee over.

The doorbell rang.

'Well, go on,' said Fifty's mum. Fifty ran up the garden and let the kitchen door slam. There was a pause before we heard voices – man voices. Fifty appeared, followed by a tall body with its face in shadow – it was Patrick or maybe Louis. Followed by Louis, or maybe Patrick. That wasn't what I was expecting.

'Hello,' shouted Fifty's mum.

'Hi,' said one twin and then the other.

'Hello, everyone,' said Bee's mum, who was carrying a big oval plate. Bee's dad was there too. I waited for the next person to come through the doorway, which was bound to be Bee. Except there was no other person. *Had they come to tell us Bee hated us? Had Bee sent them over to say we weren't friends any more?* If only I'd stayed awake I'd have known what was going on.

'What's going on?' I said to no one in particular.

'You've been abducted by aliens,' said Fifty. 'They've stolen the bodies of people you know to lure you into their world. The alien eel they placed on your earlobe is boring its way into your brain slowly taking over all your thoughts. Soon you won't know who you are, or were. You will be theirs.' Fifty is quite keen on making up ridiculous stuff. It's quite annoying.

WEIRD THINGS TRIBERS' THINK ABOUT

FIFTY: Crazy things happening, like time travel, or finding treasure, or a fairy in the Tribehouse. And making a huge fire that burns for days.

COPPER PIE: Food.

BEE: How to save all endangered species from extinction, and make people get rid of their massive cars, and stop litter and sea pollution, and on and on . . .

> *JONNO:* What else might live in the rotting tree stump that he hasn't seen yet.
>
> *KEENER:* Worrying about what might go wrong (but trying not to).

'Anyone normal going to fill me in?'

Jonno did. 'Fifty's mum told Bee's mum all about the party. Bee's mum said she'd think of a way to get Bee round here without ruining the surprise.'

'And then we cooked up a plan,' said Fifty's mum, clearly excited. 'As soon as Bee left the house to walk round here —'

'We got in the motor and here we are,' said Bee's dad, finishing off the tale.

OK, I'd got it. It was still a surprise, but a bigger one: Tribers, Probably Rose, Fifty's mum, my dad, Bee's brothers, Bee's mum and dad. Cool!

Bee's Birthday Surprise
. . . At Last

We heard footsteps and dogsteps coming along the path.
We heard them stop. Doodle's head came through the
Tribe catflap first. He barked. Bee's head followed and then
stopped, half in, half out. She stayed half in, half out.

'Get in here, Bee,' said Jonno. 'We've been working all
day and waiting all evening.'

That did it. She shuffled forwards. When she was
upright we all cheered. Her face went Keener's-face colour
– most unusual for cool-as-a-cucumber Bee.

'Happy Birthday, Bee,' said Fifty's mum above the polka
music or whatever it was. There was some random birthday-
greetings shouting and then it was party time. It was like
my dream, but better. We all sat round the rug and ate
sandwiches, crisps, pork pies, vol-au-vents (Jonno said

that's what the pastry things were) and antipasto (Bee's mum's platter of meat and cheese and olives). The twins were funny, just like they were at Bee's first birthday party, before the friends, the noise and the police. (And they apologised about Teapot, Rasher, Bodger and Slim.) You could tell Bee – the most important person – was really, really happy. There was no lost dog, her family were all together and not rowing, she wasn't in the middle of a crisis, she was just having a good time with her family and her mates – chatting and laughing and being bossy.

'Time to smack the star,' said Dad. We all jumped up, ready to whack the piñata as hard as possible. The stick was a bit bendy but after a few goes we got the idea, but we couldn't crack the clay. We whipped the star, but it would not give us the sweets. Dad had a go. Bee's dad had a go. Patrick had a go, and nearly decapitated his mum. Louis had a go, and nearly decapitated himself. No way was that clay pot going to break. Until Copper Pie decided it was time to stop messing. He did the most enormous swing, and chucked the stick plus himself at the star. It gave a little. You couldn't call it a crack, but there was a seam across the middle of the star.

'My turn, I think,' said Bee. We all stood in a ring and watched. Bee copied the Copper Pie method of piñata assassination. She swivelled round a couple of times like a hammer thrower and then let rip. It was very effective. She smashed the piñata into a zillion pieces. Sweets showered the garden like the best rainstorm ever. We all dived, and only just avoided crushing Probably Rose, who could suddenly walk much more quickly.

'Don't panic. There is cake,' said Fifty's mum. She looked a bit appalled at the headless-chicken chasing of the last few toffees.

'Give me a second.' Dad disappeared into the Tribe-house to light the candles. We could see the flickering lights through the plastic windows.

'In you come,' he shouted. Bee went first and sat on the bench. The other Tribers followed, except Fifty whose seat is the safe. The twins stood hunched over in the corner, because they're taller than the hut. Dad and Fifty's mum did the same in another corner and Bee's mum and dad filled the other two corners. Probably Rose sat down in the middle of everyone. We started singing and Bee puffed out the candles. There was a big *Hurrah!*

'Make a wish,' said Bee's dad. She shut her eyes. As soon as they opened again, Dad let the net go and balloons floated about, sinking and rising and hovering around our heads. It was brilliant. There's something about balloons that makes everyone want to bat them about. So that's what we did until it got too hot. We spilled out of the hut, red and sweaty, and let the balloons come with us and fly up in the air. We ate the fancy cake and drank the jelly Mum made because there were no spoons.

'OK,' said Dad. I thought he was going to say we should

be going but he said, 'Let's all say something we like about Bee. I'll start.' Dad looked around at the ten faces. 'I like Bee because she has definite views about all sorts of important issues, like organic farming and endangered animals.'

There was clapping.

Fifty's mum went next. 'I like the fact that she doesn't just have strong views, she acts on them, like picking up rubbish wherever she goes.'

The next few were cringe-worthy. Bee put her head down. I didn't blame her. Patrick and Louis stood up together and said how cute she was when she was little. Bee's dad told a great long story about how she behaved really badly at dinner in a restaurant one evening and in the end the waiter served her food to her under the table.

Fifty copped out and said, 'She's our mate.' (That's when I realised I was going to have to say something too. Everything I thought of sounded lame.)

Bee's mum said something in Italian and her eyes went all teary. When she'd finished they had a family hug, which was excruciatingly embarrassing. I'm so glad we're not a family-hug family.

Jonno went next. 'I like Bee loads because she lets me share her dog.' Everyone laughed. Much better than hugging.

Only Copper Pie, me . . . and Rose left. *Help!*

Copper Pie did a little cough. 'Bee's no use at football.' (Quiet laughter.) 'She eats rabbit food.' (More laughing.) 'She's mum to a Black Rhino. Doesn't like guns.' (Copper

Pie stopped for a second, then shrugged his shoulders.) 'I don't know why I like her.'

Everyone loved it. Bee did a fist of friendship in mid-air.

Rose obviously wasn't about to string together the few words she knew, so it was me next. I couldn't decide whether to try and be funny like C.P., or quick like Fifty, or say something I really meant. So I just opened my mouth . . . 'Well . . . we're a team, and we've all got jobs. Fifty is smooth-talker, Copper Pie is secret weapon, I'm the sensible one, Jonno has the most ideas, and Bee . . .' I shrugged. 'She's the boss.' I was going to say something else but there was clapping so I shut up. Bee flicked her fringe sideways and gave me a wink. Guess she liked what I said.

Fifty's mum picked up Rose, whose face was smeared with a selection of brown party foods. 'Do you want to give Bee a kiss?' *Yuck! A Rose special.* (Rose's idea of a kiss is to open her mouth and press her wet tongue against your skin. I had one once. Never again.)

I thought it was all over, but Bee wasn't ready for the party to end.

'My turn now,' she said. Not surprising – after all, Bee *is* boss. 'I've forgiven the Tribers for not answering my texts and I've forgiven my brothers for having awful friends who ruin everything, because if I hadn't been on my own all day I wouldn't have the exciting news that I've got.' All eyes were on Bee. 'With my birthday money from Nonna I've adopted a Bactrian, called Nonna.' When Bee said that I didn't think *You're a nutter, I'd have bought a mountainboard*, I thought, *That's why Tribe is the best.* We're all completely different, but together we make something better than when we're on our own. It's like we fit.

TRIBERS' BEST CAUSES AND SLOGANS

BEE: Adopt a Bactrian and save a species.

COPPER PIE: ManU for European Champions.

FIFTY: Children need sugar.

KEENER: To all forgetful swimmers, keep leaving your pounds for Keener's mountainboard fund. (Not exactly snappy.).

JONNO: Keep me here! If my parents want to move three hundred miles away, which they seem to do every twelve months, I'm staying with the Tribers.

'Come on,' said Dad. 'Time to go. Thanks, everyone.' Dad came through the Tribe flap with me. On the other side of the fence he stood up, brushed the dirt off his knees, and said, 'I wish I was a Triber.'

Dream on, Dad! No one can leave and no one can join.

Red-Handed

Hissy Fit

Last lesson on Tuesday was art. We were meant to be planning a Mondrian-type painting. (Mondrian was a famous Dutch artist.) Miss Walsh tried to explain how he used a white background, and then painted black lines down and across to make boxes and filled some of them in using three primary colours. I couldn't work out what was so clever about that. Probably Rose could manage a Mondrian if you gave her a ruler and a few crayons. Miss Walsh asked us to do a rough drawing on scrap paper before we did the real thing. Simple. Anything to do with straight lines is my kind of art!

As soon as she finished talking we all got paper and

pencils and started designing our Mondrian copies. But Jamie headed straight for the paint. He picked up the red, shook it to see if it was full and accidentally sprayed it all over the counter where Year 4's Egyptian masks were waiting to be taken home. They looked blood-spattered. (I remember when we did our Egyptian mask project. It took weeks to design and mould out of clay and fire and paint and lacquer and blah and blah and still mine turned out like a grey and brown tortoise.)

'Jamie, what on earth are you doing with that?' Miss Walsh stormed over to where he was standing holding the bottle of paint, looking dim – his usual face.

'It came out,' he said.

She undid the messy ponytail thing on her head and retied it – she was stressy. 'You shouldn't have even had your hands *on* the paint.'

'It's art. And we're painting, aren't we?' Jamie used a sarcastic voice. Not a great idea. And not quite like Jamie. He may shout out, never put up his hand, and generally be a bit of a pain, but he's not usually rude to a teacher. Even Callum, his best buddy, looked shocked.

'No, Jamie, we're not. Look around you. What is everyone else doing?' He didn't look around. He looked straight at Miss Walsh. She didn't like that.

'Sit down!' she shouted. He plonked the bottle down on the edge, knocking one of the masks, and stomped over to his desk. He folded his arms – no pencil, no paper, no Mondrian.

Art was turning out a bit more exciting than normal.

I got on with my lines and boxes. Miss Walsh got on with clearing up the mess. I showed her my sketch – not because I'm a keener, but because that's what she said to do.

'Good,' she said, without looking. That meant it was painting time. We were using A3 white paper, but I decided my Mondrian was going to be square, mostly because I like using the guillotine. It was a good move because it gave me the best view of the fight that was about to erupt between Jamie and Alice.

Alice had chosen some orange paper halfway down the paper pile. She was holding the corner trying to edge it out without upsetting all the other pieces on top. Jamie came over and got hold of another corner of the same piece of paper. Odd, as we were meant to be using white.

'That's mine,' said Alice. 'Mi-iss!'

Miss Walsh took no notice.

Jamie gave the paper a tug. Alice tugged too. It was going to tear, obviously. It was just a question of when. The paper pile started to lean. Alice tried to stop it with her free hand. Jamie didn't seem to care about the pile. He was fighting to the death. Multi-coloured pieces of paper floated to the floor and spread out like a rainbow, leaving the orange paper at the top of the pile. Jamie ripped it away from Alice, all except her corner. She looked at it as though her pet budgie had been torn in half and started wailing.

I'd like to repeat everything Miss Walsh said to Jamie

but there was too much of it to remember. The basic message was: *You are a complete and utter idiot and I wish you would go away and I never knew teaching would mean I had to deal with kids like you and I should have got a job in the Build-a-Bear Workshop.*

It was one of her genuine hissy fits, last seen on bring-in-your-pets day.

THE HAMSTER HISSY FIT

Fifty tripped carrying Lily's hamster and catapulted it into the bin. He tipped the bin upside down to save the creature from the pencil shavings and tissues (which it probably quite liked) and it fell out and landed on Miss Walsh's shoe and she panicked and kicked it. (Don't worry, it survived.) Lily was livid and threatened to kick Miss Walsh. Miss Walsh lost the plot. It was excellent.

The Mondrians were finished in complete silence. I liked the quiet and got very involved in my coloured boxes. When the bell went I jumped a mile. Jamie jumped too, right out of his seat, and headed for the door. That's not allowed. We're meant to wait for Miss Walsh to give us permission to pack up. He slammed the door, mega hard. Jamie was in a right temper and heading for trouble.

Oh well, nothing to do with us, I thought. As usual, I was wrong.

What Was That All About?

'Do you want to come to the café?' asked Bee after school.

'No,' said Copper Pie.

'Same,' said Fifty.

'I'll come,' said Jonno.

'What about you, Keener?' said Bee.

I weighed it up – a hot chocolate with Bee and Jonno or a snack at home, probably with Flo. Weirdly, home won.

'I'll pass,' I said.

'I've got something for Toni to say thanks for letting Doodle sleepover.' Bee reached into her bag and brought out a photo of Doodle in a frame. Not most people's idea of a gift.

'Come on, let's go,' said Jonno. We all walked down the alley together.

'What was that about with Jamie?' said Fifty.

'No idea,' said Bee. 'But it wasn't about the paint.'

'It was,' said Copper Pie.

'It was, but it wasn't,' said Jonno.

'That's clear,' said Fifty, meaning the opposite.

'The paint started it, but Jamie must have been upset about something else. He's always getting told off but he doesn't normally storm out,' said Bee.

'Maybe he's fallen out with Callum,' Fifty said.

'That would be too good to be true,' said Bee.

She went off to the café with Jonno. Copper Pie branched off to his house and Fifty and I were left on our own.

'Do you want to come to mine?' he asked.

'No, thanks.' I wanted to go home and swing in my hammock.

Or did I? Amy was wailing in the kitchen. Mum shooed me away. Something was up – big time. I waited in my room for the sobbing to stop, which took a while.

'Does anyone want some cheese biscuits?' Mum shouted up the stairs a bit later.

'I'm on my way!' I ran downstairs two steps at a time and nearly (note the 'nearly') crashed into Flo at the bottom. She'd been watching telly.

'Mu-um, Keener hurt me,' she winged.

'Did not.'

'Did.'

'Did not.'

Mum came to the kitchen door and gave us a look that stopped what she calls 'the panto'.

PANTOMIME ARGUING

You know the whole 'Behind you!' 'Where?' Behind you!' Where?' stuff that you get at the Christmas panto? Well Mum says that's what we sound like when we do the 'You did', 'I didn't' arguing, so in our house it's called 'the panto'.

We had the biscuits washed down with blackcurrant. Mum made a grave face. 'I want you to be nice to Amy,' she said.

Pigs might fly, I thought. *Fish might climb palm trees.*

'Because he dumped her, didn't he, Mummy?' said listen-at-doors Flo.

'Dumped isn't a nice word to use, Flo, but yes, they've split up.'

My grin started at one ear lobe and finished at the other. No more spotty boyfriend, no more snogging in the front room, no more Friday night suppers with the love-birds cooing at each other.

And if Jamie had split up with Callum too, then things couldn't get much better.

Breaking
News

I met Fifty on the way to school as normal. We got there
before Bee but after Copper Pie and Jonno, as normal. We
hung around on our patch, as normal. I like normal – it
means we're not in trouble.

Normal didn't last long, however. There were two odd
things in our classroom, completely unrelated. The fancy
new whiteboard had turned smeary pink, and Callum wasn't
at school. Miss Walsh didn't read out his name so she must
have known already. Mums are meant to call in if you're off
sick, so the school doesn't send the truancy officer round. I
looked round at Jamie. He looked just as angry as the last
time I saw him, marching out of the art room. Something
was definitely up.

Alice asked why the board was pink.

'There was an accident,' said Miss Walsh.

'Is it ruined?' said Alice. 'It looks ruined.'

'Geography books out, please, and turn to the maps we drew last week.' Miss Walsh didn't want to discuss the board. Pity. It was hard to imagine what made it prawn colour.

At break our patch got a bit crowded. Lily, Ed and Marco came over and joined the Tribers to deliver the breaking news, CNN-style. Lily was the newsreader with the dynamite headline.

'Callum's been suspended.' She paused for maximum dramatic effect. 'He insulted Miss Walsh.'

It was a short news bulletin, with nowhere near enough information. The news team were bombarded with questions: What did he say? When did he say it? How do you know? The answers were: Don't know. Don't know. Jamie told Ed.

'Go and find out more,' said Bee to Ed. Bee is used to being obeyed, but not this time.

'Jamie won't say anything else. He's being really strange about it all. It's like *he's* been suspended, not Callum.' The news team disappeared to tell the rest of the playground.

Break was too short. Getting rid of Callum was like a Tribe birthday present, and we couldn't stop talking about it. Copper Pie was made up. They're in the football team together. C.P. calls him Hog.

LIFE WITHOUT CALLUM

- No one would hog the ball in football, except Copper Pie, but he is captain.
- No one would spy on Tribe.
- No one would pelt us with rubbers in the classroom.
- No one would tease Fifty for being small, Keener for being wimpy, Bee for being bossy or Copper Pie for being ginger. (No one teases Jonno.)
- Tribe wouldn't have any enemies, except Jamie, who'd be useless on his own.

As we filed back into class, the main topic was the chance of suspension becoming exclusion.

'Depends what he said to her,' said Bee.

'Same,' said Fifty.

When I walked in I heard Alice say, 'I can't bear the smell, miss.' She wasn't wrong. It smelt like it came from one of those cans which has a big black cross on the back and a massive warning saying, *Only use in well ventilated areas* and gives you an instant headache. The caretaker, who is whiskery like a walrus, snarled at Alice and shuffled off.

'It'll be gone in no time,' said Miss Walsh. 'Would you please open that window, Jonno.' The smell was coming from the whiteboard, which was white again.

'What was the accident that made the board pink, Miss?' said Alice.

'Oh Alice!' She smiled. 'If only you were as interested in your work as you are in all the other aspects of what goes on in the school.' But the smile was pure venom. Jamie and Alice are the two kids in our class that drive Miss Walsh mad (followed by the Tribers).

No one played up for the whole of the rest of the morning because Miss Walsh was giving out don't-mess-with-me vibes. Callum was well out of it.

Lunchtime Update

We had sausages – everyone's favourite (except Bee's – she had a jacket potato). Jamie sat at the next table with some kids from Year 5. I almost (only almost) felt sorry for him. Having no friends is pretty grim. We cleared our table and went outside to find Lily waiting on our patch.

'Callum didn't *say* anything to Miss Walsh,' she said. 'He *wrote* something. On the whiteboard. With red paint.' She paused a few times to make the point. 'That's why it was pink. That's why Walrus was cleaning it.'

'How do you know?' said Fifty.

'Walrus told Miss Maggs, and she told me.' Miss Maggs is the playground monitor. She used to like us until Copper Pie got Jonno in a headlock. Jonno's forgiven him, but Miss Maggs doesn't believe in forgiveness.

Lily went off to tell more people. She was obviously enjoying herself. Bee disappeared after her.

'Those whiteboards are *really* expensive,' said Fifty. 'He was lucky Walrus got it off.'

'Why would Callum write something about Miss Walsh on the board in red paint?' said Jonno.

DIFFERENT REDS

- Redhead (Copper Pie)
- Red herring (a false clue)
- Reds (Liverpool F.C.)
- Red planet (Mars)
- Red-letter day (a special day)
- Blood red
- Rod Adair (famous firefighter)
- Red Arrows (aerobatic team)
- Red-handed (caught in the act)

'Don't know. Don't care,' said Copper Pie. I agreed.

'It's all quite odd,' said Jonno. 'I know Callum's got it in for us, but he doesn't go looking for trouble with teachers, or, in fact, the other kids.'

Fifty had a lightbulb moment. 'Maybe it was because of Jamie. Maybe he couldn't bear Miss Walsh being so nasty to Jamie in art yesterday and so he took revenge.'

Unlikely, I thought.

'Unlikely,' said Jonno. 'They're mates but that would be weird.'

'That would be like they were in love,' said Fifty. He started singing: 'Jamie and Callum sitting in the tree, K-I-S-S-I-N-G. First comes love —'

'Shut it,' said Copper Pie.

'I wonder what Callum wrote,' I said. The four of us spent the rest of lunch break making suggestions. Copper Pie's were rude. Mine were dull. Jonno hardly thought of any (I don't think he likes being mean) and Fifty's sounded like advertising slogans: *Miss Walsh, stress in a dress. My hair's in a bun, and I'm no fun.*

The bell went so we lined up. Bee came out of the door we were about to go through.

'Where have you been?' asked Jonno as she slipped in behind us.

'Interrogating Walrus.'

'And?' said four voices at the same time.

'Tell you later,' she said in a very serious voice with a very serious face to match. Even though I didn't really care what was going on with Callum I couldn't help being curious.

Curiouser
and Curiouser

After school Bee said, 'I'll see you at the Tribehouse,' and dashed out of the classroom door before any of us had a chance to say anything. What was she up to?

'What's Bee up to?' said Fifty.

'No idea,' I said. I looked at Jonno – he spends more time with her than we do because he sort of shares her dog. He shook his head. It was a mystery.

We turned into the alley just in time to see two figures reach the other end and vanish from view. It looked like Bee and Jamie, but I figured I needed my eyes testing because that was about as likely as me going off with Callum.

OTHER UNLIKELY EVENTS

COPPER PIE eating a green vegetable.

FIFTY deciding to swim the Channel.

JONNO killing the stag beetle that lives in our tree stump.

BEE eating beef-flavour crisps and dropping the packet.

KEENER picking a fight.

'Was that Jamie?' said Fifty.

'I think it was,' said Jonno.

I did a 'maybe' nod, which is like a nod with a wobble halfway down.

'With Bee?' added Fifty.

'Traitor,' said Copper Pie.

'Don't be an idiot,' said Fifty. 'It must be something to do with Callum. And Walrus. And maybe Jamie. And . . .'

'And we'll find out at six o'clock,' I said. 'Tribe meeting.'

'Same,' said Fifty.

I got to the Tribehouse early because I wanted to know why Bee went to talk to Walrus, and what she'd found out from him, and why she'd walked home with Jamie, second-worst person in our class, school, world, universe, etc. The others had the same idea. We were all ready and waiting ten minutes before the meeting was due to start.

'Maybe Jamie's kidnapped Bee and is torturing her to find out all the Tribe secrets,' said Fifty.

We all ignored him. He didn't shut up.

'Maybe Bee has been sprayed with a chemical, the chemical Walrus used on the whiteboard, and the side-effect is that you fall in love with your enemy's deputy.'

'I like walruses,' said Jonno, He gave us a lecture on them while we waited for Bee. It was better than listening to Fifty.

WHY WALRUSES ARE GREAT

Their tusks, which are their canine teeth, grow a metre long. They use them to haul themselves out of the water and to break holes in the ice from underneath and to fight. They're hugely fat, because they need all the blubber to keep warm, and their heart rate is mega-slow which helps them survive the icy water. Their whiskers are really clever detection devices to find their favourite dinner – shellfish. Their suction is so strong – better than a Dyson – that they can suck a baby seal's brain out through its nose. They live about forty years, weigh as much as 1.5 tons and make lots of noise – mainly snorts and bellows. The scientific name for walrus is Odobenus Rosmarus, which means tooth-walking sea-horse.

We heard Doodle bark and Bee's head poked in the door.

'Hi,' she said.

'Go on,' said Fifty. 'Spill.'

'OK,' she said. 'You know Lily told us that Callum had painted on the board.' We all nodded. 'Well that made me remember something I'd sort of forgotten, something I noticed, but didn't know was going to be important.' She lowered her voice. 'When Jamie stormed out of art, I saw him shove the red paint up his sweatshirt.' She stopped, moved aside her great big fringe, and looked around, making sure we all understood the point. 'And that made me wonder how they knew it was *Callum*, and not *Jamie*, who wrote on the board.' She had her hands on her hips – it makes her look like she's boss.

'Jamie could have given it to Callum,' I said.

'Maybe,' she said. 'But that's why I went to talk to Walrus. I wanted to know how they knew it was Callum.'

'And?' I said. It was like a murder mystery. Colonel Mustard in the conservatory with the lead piping.

'Callum was caught in the classroom by Walrus. He'd come to mend that window that gets stuck. Callum was standing there on his own and he had red paint on his sweatshirt.'

'So Jamie gave Callum the paint,' said Jonno.

'There wasn't any bottle of paint,' said Bee. 'Not anywhere. I asked him that.'

'Who cares?' said Copper Pie.

'I care,' said Bee. 'Because it doesn't make any sense. I don't believe Callum would write something about Miss Walsh on the whiteboard with red paint.'

'I think the police would disagree. The guilty party was caught red-handed, red-sweatshirted, in fact. Case closed,' said Fifty.

'Red-sweatshirted but no paint bottle anywhere,' said Bee.

'Bee's thinking more Sherlock Holmes than local cop, aren't you, Bee?' Jonno grinned at her. Sometimes I think they have a mini club of their own with a language we don't understand. I had no idea what he meant but I didn't ask because I didn't want to look stupid. Luckily Copper Pie didn't mind looking stupid.

'What you on about?'

Jonno sighed as though it was hard explaining things to idiots like us. 'Sherlock Holmes didn't go looking for obvious clues like blood, or a bullet, or red paint, he sort of studied people's behaviour and knew all sorts of random facts and totally odd things that helped him solve crimes.' Jonno moved his glasses up his nose and actually looked through them for once. 'Like he could tell from the mud on a shoe where in London that shoe had walked – with a leg in it, of course.'

I was following the Sherlock thing but didn't see what it had to do with Bee's idea that Callum was innocent. Fifty did though.

'So you think a normal sort of detective would accuse Callum because of the paint on his sweatshirt and because he was in the classroom, but a Sherlock-type of detective would think about the fact that Callum had no reason to be cross with Miss Walsh and would look for another explanation for the fact he was covered with red paint and standing by the board with something rude written in red paint.'

'Yes,' said Bee and Jonno together.

Smug pair, I thought.

'Did you ask Jamie if *he* did it?' said Fifty.

Bee shook her head. 'No, of course not. I asked him if Callum was all right. I wanted to see if he looked guilty about Callum being suspended.'

'And did he?' said Jonno.

'Not that I could tell,' said Bee. 'He looked really unhappy, but I'm not convinced that means anything. I asked him if he knew why Callum did it – even though I'm sure he didn't – to see what he'd say but he just shrugged. I couldn't get much out of him. It was like talking to a dummy in a shop window.'

'How long's Callum been chucked out for?' said Copper Pie.

'Till he confesses, according to Jamie,' said Bee.

'So that means he says he didn't do it,' I said.

'Exactly,' said Bee. 'Because it wasn't him. And we need to prove it.'

'Why?' said Copper Pie.

'Because it's not right,' said Bee. I didn't want to get involved, but Jonno was nodding so that meant two Tribers were on a mission to save the dreaded Callum and two Tribers meant all the Tribers. I waited to hear what the plan was.

No Way, Never

'No way,' said Copper Pie. 'No way.' He said it again in case we hadn't understood.

'Callum won't bite,' said Bee.

'He might,' said Fifty. I didn't say anything. The idea that Tribe was planning to go round and see Callum hadn't quite managed to penetrate the bit of my brain that thinks. It was like the Jedi popping round to see the Sith.

'I'm with Bee,' said Jonno. 'It's serious being suspended. And if it wasn't actually him, that's not right. If Callum's not guilty, someone needs to sort this out.'

But why us? my brain was shouting.

'OK,' said Fifty. 'Why don't we see if Callum's at school tomorrow? If he's not, we'll go round after school. If he is, it must mean someone else has sorted it out.'

'I'm not going. Full stop.' That was all Copper Pie had to say about it. And it stopped us as well. We moved on to more interesting stuff, like the next Tribe road trip. We all went surfing with my dad one Sunday and everyone was keen to do it again, even Fifty who's not mad about water but liked the hot chocolate, the bacon sarnies and the KitKats.

'My dad wants to come next time,' said Bee.

'We don't want any more dads,' said Copper Pie.

'Same,' said Fifty. 'Loads of us and one dad is best.'

'Tell your dad to organise his own surf trip,' said Copper Pie.

'I'll tell him you said so,' said Bee and stuck out her tongue. That's all it took. A Tribe war broke out which involved pushing and shoving and teasing and then laughing. Meeting over. We did the handshake and left the hut.

On the way home I thought about Callum. If I was suspended, Mum or Dad would have to stay home to look after me. It would probably be Dad because he can work from home but Mum couldn't (unless she invited her patients into our kitchen). If I was at home with Dad and he quizzed me for more than about ten minutes I'd end up confessing everything. So surely Callum's parents would get the truth out of him too. And if it wasn't him that wrote rude words on the whiteboard with red paint, then his parents would find out and they'd tell the school. By the time I got home I was pretty sure that there wouldn't be any need to go visiting the enemy.

Enemy
Territory

Callum wasn't at school. Jamie didn't do any shouting out all day. Jamie didn't do anything all day as far as I could tell, except stare at his desk. Bee did plenty. She found out where Callum lives – we knew the road but not the number – and talked us through what she was going to say. Our job was to leave the talking to her. Simple. Except Copper Pie wouldn't come.

'Go without me,' he said.

'Come on, it's not the same if we don't all go,' said Fifty. We were in the playground. School had finished ages ago but we were still trying to convince Copper Pie that he had to come to Callum's with us.

'I've told you. I don't like him. I don't care if he did it or not. I DON'T CARE.' Copper Pie walked off towards the gates. Jonno did few skips to catch up. The rest of us followed, but quite far behind.

'Looks like it's just the four of us then,' said Fifty.

Bee sighed. I think she was disappointed in C.P. I was disappointed that I hadn't thought of saying the same as him. I didn't want to go to Callum's either.

'What if Callum's dad's there?' asked Fifty.

'What if he is?' said Bee.

'He might send us away.'

'Why would he do that? You're such a wimp, Fifty.'

And you're a bit of a bully sometimes, Bee, I thought. And that thought stayed well inside.

At the end of the alley, Jonno and Copper Pie turned right towards Callum's. Home for all of us is left. I looked at Bee and Fifty with raised eyebrows. They raised their eyebrows back at me. We jogged to catch up. Bee and I went to one side, Fifty went to the other. Copper Pie was surrounded.

'Are you coming, then?' said Fifty.

'Looks like it,' said Copper Pie. Jonno had obviously worked some magic. He's good at persuading people, also known as brainwashing.

Callum's house was only three minutes from school. We slowed down as we got nearer, and made a V-formation like birds do, with Bee in the lead in the middle at the front, Jonno one side, Fifty the other and me and Copper Pie behind on the wings. Callum's house didn't have a front garden, the front door was on the pavement. Bee knocked three times. We

156

waited for the enemy to open the door and let us in.

'What are you doing here?' said the blond head poking round the door. He didn't open it all the way. Maybe he thought we'd charge in and attack him.

'We've come because we don't think it was you who painted on the whiteboard,' said Bee. She was straight to the point. Callum didn't seem to know what to say.

'Is your dad in?' said Fifty. What a stupid thing to ask.

Callum shook his head, opened the door a bit more and said, 'Are you coming in?'

No, I thought.

'Yes, thanks,' said Bee.

Callum turned first right off the hall into the telly room. That gameshow with money in red boxes was on. He pressed mute. I watched anyway.

'Walrus told me you got caught with red paint on your sweatshirt,' said Bee.

'So?' said Callum.

'So, I've been thinking, and I don't think you were writing, I think you might have been cleaning it off.' There was a long silence. I was busy thinking that Bee's idea sounded quite believable. Callum seemed to be busy deciding what to say. Everyone else was either busy waiting, or watching the moving mouths on the telly.

'What if I was?' said Callum eventually.

'Why would you let everyone believe you're guilty if you're not?' said Bee.

157

'Unless you're protecting someone else,' said Jonno. (It was like watching Sherlock Holmes and Doctor Watson in action.)

'What if I am?' said Callum.

'We know it's Jamie,' said Bee. (There isn't exactly a long list of people Callum could call friends.)

'What if it is?'

'It's not fair for you to take the blame,' said Jonno.

Callum used a sarcastic voice. 'So the Tribe think I should tell on him, do they?' It was a good question. We wouldn't tell on each other so why should Callum tell on Jamie? No one had the answer.

Bee went off in another direction with her interrogation. 'Why did he do it?'

'He hates Miss Walsh. And she hates him.'

'Are you sure that's all?' Bee moved her fringe – always a sign that things are getting serious. 'Is there something else?' Callum didn't look like he was about to speak so she carried on. 'There must be a reason why he gets told off every day for years and one day, that's no worse than loads of others, he storms out of class and writes something on the whiteboard with red paint.'

'Ask him,' said Callum.

I heard a key in the lock. 'Hello!' shouted someone that I assumed was Callum's mum. She came in and smiled at us. She didn't look anything like our mums. She was wearing a dark trouser suit and a shirt and looked like a newsreader. And she had a briefcase.

'Hello,' said Jonno. 'I'm Jonno . . . from school.'

'Come to see the graffiti artist, have you?' She tutted.

We did some nodding. There was an awkward gap. Fifty filled it.

'We came to see how he was.' It sounded like Callum was ill.

'I expect he's bored having spent all day at home,' said his mum. 'Anyway, I need to get changed and then I'm nipping round to Karen's.' She headed out of the door. 'You can all stay for tea if you like. Cheer him up.'

'They're going,' said Callum.

Too right, tea with the enemy was out of the question.

'You can come with me then, Callum,' his mum shouted from the staircase. 'Karen's not so good, the latest treatment's knocked her for six, so I may as well make Jamie and Katy their tea and you can eat with them.'

'OK,' said Callum.

'We'd better go,' said Bee. We followed our leader out of the room, except Copper Pie who was glued to the mute telly. Fifty grabbed his elbow and pulled him along. Bee opened the front door and we all trooped past her and started heading back the way we'd come, but she stayed where she was.

'Are you coming?' said Fifty.

'You go on,' she shouted. 'I'll catch up.' I could tell that she was on to something. We waited to hear the latest from the Tribe detective.

There Are No Right Answers

We hung around at the end of the alley waiting for Bee.

'So how come you changed your mind and came to Callum's, Copper Pie?' said Fifty.

'Jonno made me,' said Copper Pie. He flashed Jonno a mean look. I laughed. Jonno couldn't make C.P. do anything.

'How exactly did he make you?' said Fifty. 'Chinese burn?'

Copper Pie kicked some imaginary dirt on the pavement. Jonno was smiling, waiting to hear what he was going to say. Copper Pie spoke to the floor. 'Jonno said I owed it to you for what happened at the summer fair.'

I would never have dared mention Copper Pie going off with Callum to do the football stall at the summer fair. That was all in the past. Thankfully Bee wasn't long. I didn't want to go over the whole episode that threatened Tribe's existence ever again.

'I guessed right,' she said. (There's a surprise.) 'It wasn't Callum. It was Jamie. But there's nothing we can do about it.'

'Did Callum actually say it was Jamie?' asked Fifty.

'He didn't need to. I know it was Jamie, and I know why he did it, and I know why Callum's covering up for him.' Bee is *such* a know-all.

'Tell us then,' said Fifty.

'Miss Walsh telling him off was the last straw for Jamie, because he's really upset. His mum's got cancer.' She paused to make sure we knew that was bad. 'That's why Callum doesn't want to land him in it. That's why Callum tried to rub off the writing before anyone found out. That's how he got his sweatshirt covered in paint. And that's where he and his mum are going now. To Jamie's.'

'How do you know?' I asked.

'Jamie's sister's called Katy, so I knew it was his mum that isn't well. And did you notice Callum's mum said "treatment"? Everyone knows what that means.'

'In our house it would mean Mum's gone for a pedicure,' said Jonno.

'It would be physio in mine,' I said.

Fifty made the my-mum's-a-loony face. 'And we'd be meditating in mine, with joss sticks.'

We all looked at Copper Pie. 'A telling off. Definitely.'

'Well, in Jamie's house it means cancer treatment,' said

Bee. 'I asked Callum straight out and he nodded, but he'd promised Jamie he wouldn't tell anyone. Jamie doesn't want anyone to know. And neither does his mum.'

Bee put her fist out for the fist of friendship. We knew what that meant – keep the secret.

'So . . . Callum's innocent, but unless he dumps Jamie in it he's got no way of proving it.'

'Exactly,' said Bee. 'So what do we do?'

'Nothing,' said Copper Pie. 'It's not our problem.' I was about to agree but . . .

'That's so mean,' said Bee. 'We may not like him but Callum can't stay off school forever for something he didn't do.'

'Has he told his mum the truth?' I asked. 'Surely she could sort it out with Miss Walsh or the Head.' My solutions usually rely on other people. I like it that way.

'He can't have done, can he? Didn't you hear her call him a "graffiti artist"?' Bee was right, as usual.

I had another try. 'Why can't we just tell Miss Walsh the truth? She's not going to come down hard on Jamie when she knows about the . . . you know.'

'It's called cancer, Keener. You can't catch it by saying it.'

'I know,' I said.

Jonno pushed his springy hair off his face, and it sprang back to where it started. 'The thing is, if we say Jamie did it, even if he doesn't get suspended it'll make everything much worse for him.'

'Much worse for his mum,' said Bee. 'If she feels rubbish already, how will she feel if she knows Jamie's going around spraying insults all over school.'

'One whiteboard, Bee. Not all over school,' I said. She ignored me.

'There must be a way we can get Callum in the clear without dropping anyone else in it,' said Jonno.

'This is mad,' said Copper Pie. 'We hate Hog.'

'It's not about Callum,' said Jonno. Seemed to me that it was, but I waited to hear what Jonno thought. 'It's about what's fair.'

I hate it when people say things like 'fair' or 'right'. It always means we have to do something we don't want to.

'And it's about us as well,' said Bee. 'About being Tribe. We don't go around not caring about the rest of the world, do we?' There was a bit of reluctant nodding from me and Fifty, and agreeing-type nodding from Jonno, and a completely still head from Copper Pie, which Bee pretended not to notice.

'OK. We've agreed that we're getting Callum off the hook. All we need is a plan that doesn't involve Jamie. Thinking caps on.'

The Tribe's
Thinking Caps

Copper Pie: Let's say someone else did it.

Bee: We can't dump on some poor innocent kid.

Fifty: We could say we saw who did it but didn't recognise him.

Keener: We could say we know Callum didn't do it but we don't know who did.

Jonno: But in that case how would they know Callum's telling the truth?

Keener: We know he's telling the truth. Bee said.

Jonno: We know, but how does Miss Walsh or whoever know?

Bee: It's no good just saying Callum's innocent. We need evidence.

Fifty: Let's give him an alibi.

Bee: But we don't know when it happened.

Fifty: A long alibi then. From the end of art until bedtime.

Copper Pie: No one would believe that.

Jonno: What about using the right to remain silent?

Keener: What's that?

Fifty: It's what filthy rich criminals do. They refuse to answer questions.

Jonno: And they get their lawyers to get them off.

Bee: How does that help us?

Jonno: We say we know who did it but we can't tell anyone.

Fifty: Can you see the Head letting us get away with that?

Keener: Even worse, she'd think it was a Triber.

Bee: She can think what she likes. We're not covered in red paint.

Jonno: OK. Unless someone comes up with something better —

Bee: Before break tomorrow.

Jonno: We're choosing to use our right to remain silent.

Bee: Only partly silent.

Fifty: And partly loud.

Keener: Partly very annoying, to Miss Walsh.

Copper Pie: Totally mad.

Jonno: And completely Tribish.

A Chat
With Dad

I was still awake when Dad got home from Timbuctoo or wherever it is he goes to work. He poked his head in, which he says he always does but as I'm asleep I've never known if he was telling the truth or not.

'Hi, Dad,' I said, quietly.

He came and sat on the edge of my bed. 'How's things?' he whispered back.

'OK.'

'Something keeping you awake?'

'Sort of.'

'Anything you want to share?'

I thought for a second before I decided to tell Dad everything. If it was Mum who had asked I'd have kept it to myself because she might have made me tell on Jamie but I was pretty sure Dad wouldn't. He listened to the story from the beginning – pink whiteboard and missing Callum – through the middle – Walrus and Bee, Bee and Jamie, Tribe and Callum – to the finale – telling Miss Walsh it wasn't Callum but refusing to tell her how we knew or who the real graffiti artist was. Dad took it all in.

'Whose idea was it to use the right to remain silent?'

'Jonno's,' I said.

'That figures,' said Dad. 'Smart boy.' Everyone likes Jonno.

'Do you think it will work?'

'Depends what you mean,' said Dad. 'I think they'll have to listen to you, and they'll probably believe you because you're no friend of Callum's so you wouldn't be sticking up for him out of loyalty.' There was a pause. I helped Dad along.

'But?'

'But I think they'll insist you name the guilty party.'

'They can't make us.' I sounded braver than I felt. I wasn't keen on the word 'insist'.

'Hold onto that thought,' said Dad. 'They can't make you. And I won't either. Seems like Jamie and his mum have got enough to deal with.' Dad got up to leave, but stopped at the door.

'It wouldn't hurt to let Jamie know you've figured it all out, but you're not going to rat on him. It won't help anyone if he takes what's happening with his mum out on people at school.'

'OK,' I said. 'Thanks, Dad.' I didn't want to forget what Dad said so I hopped out of bed and wrote down the important bits.

They can't make us tell on Jamie.

But we need to tell Jamie we know.

Showdown

I overslept on Friday. Oversleeping in our house isn't normally possible because there are five of us and three of them set alarms. But Dad switched his off because he was working from home, which meant he didn't have to get up and out by seven. The one on Mum's side of the bed went off extra early because she was going on a course, but she didn't wake up Flo and me because she'd asked Amy to get us up. Amy uses her iPhone and she forgot that she'd put it on silent because spotty boyfriend's been calling her all the time – he's changed his mind and wants her back. *Don't do it, Amy.* So, Dad came charging in at eight-thirty, ripped my duvet off and yelled in my ear.

I yelled too. *Waaaaagh!* Not because I was late, because I was frightened.

Dad drove us all to school. I'd missed registration.

'Sorry I'm late, miss.'

I had a quick check. Callum wasn't there. So the show-down was still set for break. I repeated in my head the main bits of my chat with Dad. All I had to do was keep my gob shut when Miss Walsh demanded to know who the poison-painter was.

Time whizzed by. The bell went and instead of legging it outside, the others stayed in the classroom so I did too. I wished I'd been in on the discussions before school. I didn't know what the plan was.

'Miss Walsh, can we talk to you please?' said Bee.

Miss Walsh bundled her books up. 'Not now, Bee. See me after break.' She left.

Bee sat back on one of the desks. 'Great!'

'It doesn't matter. We'll tell her after break,' said Jonno.

We decided to stay inside. It's not allowed but that way we'd be there when Miss Walsh got back and before all the rest of our class came in from break. It was a bad move. Break is short, but break doing nothing but waiting for your stressy teacher is extremely long.

Finally we heard the clip-clop of Miss Walsh's red shoes. She wears high heels and sticky-out flowery skirts. Bee says she looks like a little girl wearing her mum's clothes.

'So what is it?' she said as she came in. 'Another spon-sored silence? Another endangered animal found in your tree stump?' Something told me Miss Walsh wasn't in the mood to hear our announcement. Bee hesitated before she launched into the speech she'd rehearsed.

'We know that Callum's been suspended for writing on the whiteboard, but we also know he didn't do it. We know who did do it, and so does Callum, but we can't tell you the name. We have the right to remain silent, about that bit, but Callum needs to be allowed back to school because he is completely innocent.' The first members of our class started trickling back in, in time to hear Miss Walsh's response.

'Who do you think you are? The school's conscience? Callum's situation is *nothing* to do with you. And neither is his guilt or innocence. Let's hope the senior school knocks some of the hot air out of you. Something needs to. Sit down, the lot of you.'

I went to sit down, but I stopped before I got to my chair because none of the other Tribers had moved. They were standing in a row, looking gob-smacked. Bee recovered first.

'So you don't care that Callum is at home accused of something he didn't do?' she said. The rest of the class were enjoying the spat but I wanted to crawl into my desk. Angry Bee is quite scary. And Angry Bee usually gets us all in deep trouble.

'Don't talk to me like that,' said Miss Walsh.

'What's going on here?' said a voice I'd rather not have heard at that particular moment – the Head's.

Miss Walsh opened her mouth but Bee was quicker.

'We have just told Miss Walsh that we *know* who wrote on the whiteboard with paint, although we can't say who it was, but it *wasn't* Callum. And Miss Walsh said —'

'Enough,' said the Head. 'I don't think this is a conversation the whole class needs to hear. My office, you five.' She looked at the four Tribers in a row, I think she might even have counted them to make doubly sure there were only four, and then she spotted me, hovering near my desk. She pointed. 'That includes you.'

The Head turned to our livid teacher, who was about to have a hissy fit that matched the kicking-the-hamster one. 'I'll handle this, thank you, Miss Walsh.'

Not again! I wanted to scream. Why were the Tribers always in the Head's office? Because of Bee was the answer this time, and a few other times. *Her mouth needs a zip*, I thought. *A lockable one.*

On the way I remembered Dad's words about the right to remain silent. *No one can make us say anything.* I repeated it in my head, to make sure it stuck.

Saying Nothing

I was last through the Head's door. I turned round to shut it and I'm sure I saw the back of Callum's mum disappearing out of the main door. When I turned back round the Head was smiling. Spooky.

"Thank you, Keener."

Bee tried to carry on from where she left off. 'We —' but the Head stopped her after the first syllable.

'I don't think you are very fond of Callum, and vice versa,' she said, doing her usual swivelling round to include us all. 'But I find I'm not surprised to hear you pleading his case. A sense of what's right seems to run very deep with your Tribe.' She was still smiling. It was unnerving. 'As you already know, it wasn't Callum who damaged the white-board. Although the evidence certainly pointed that way.'

Still smiling. 'I gather from Callum's mother that it was after your visit that Callum told her the truth. I don't think we need discuss who was to blame – that truth shall stay unspoken between those who know, for reasons we also know.' Listening to the Head made me feel like we were part of a secret society. One that smiled a lot.

Everyone nodded, so I did too.

'Leave it to me,' said the Head, and stood up, which meant it was time to go. 'And good work,' she added.

'Thank you,' said Jonno. I was already in the corridor so I didn't say anything. In fact, I'd said nothing throughout the whole showdown. Perfect!

We didn't go straight back to our class. We loitered in the corridor and whispered about how amazing it is that just when we think we're in sinking sand up to our necks, somehow someone throws the Tribers a rope and we drag ourselves out.

'Let's go back in now. Miss Walsh will be expecting us to look defeated. This will finish her off,' said Bee.

'Don't rub it in, Bee,' said Jonno.

Why not? I thought.

'Why not? She said she didn't care,' said Bee.

'*You* said she didn't care,' said Jonno. '*She* said it was nothing to do with us.'

'Whatever.' Bee pushed open the classroom door.

'In you come,' said Miss Walsh, peculiarly nicely. 'We're having a quiet few minutes listening to some of Siegfried

Sassoon's poetry from World War One.'

We filed in and sat down. Miss Walsh read a poem called 'Everybody Sang'. She read it twice. Afterwards she asked what it was about. Jonno was really into it. He said, 'He's talking about freedom and letting go, or maybe being let go.' I thought it was about singing so I didn't say anything. Jamie put his hand up and shouted at the same time, 'It's the end of the war.'

For once Miss Walsh let him off. She said, 'Very good, Jamie. The poem was written after the Armistice, when the horror of war was over.'

It seemed to me that it wasn't just Callum that was in the clear. Jamie looked a whole lot happier. It must have been pretty difficult for him, knowing his mate was suspended for something he did. But I could understand why he hadn't owned up. If your mum had, you know, then you wouldn't want her to be any more upset, would you?

I didn't think we needed to take Dad's advice and make sure Jamie knew that we knew. Callum's mum had sorted all that out by telling the Head about the paint and the problem at home. And Miss Walsh knew too – that was obvious. So, Tribe's job was over . . .

. . . Almost

Jonno rang as I was about to go out of the door with the rest of my family. On Friday nights we all go out to supper as a treat. We take turns choosing where we go. This week it was Amy. I didn't care where we went. I was just pleased that spotty face wasn't coming too. I hope she never gets another boyfriend.

'Keener, what are you doing Saturday night?'

What did he expect me to say? Going to a night club or a pub, going out dancing with my girlfriend . . .

'Nothing,' I said.

'Not any more, you're not. We're going out.' It sounded a bit odd. Like I was going out with Jonno. I waited, which doesn't work that well on the telephone. He spoke again. 'We're all meeting at the Tribehouse at five o'clock.'

'Who's we?' I said.

'The Tribers, of course.'

'OK. And where are we going?' I was hoping it was Bee's.

'See you then.' He put the phone down.

'Come on,' said Amy. I was last in the car but Amy and Flo had both sat in the outside seats so I had to clamber over and sit in the middle. There should be a rule that stops that happening.

'Where are we going?'

'Prego,' said Amy. Good. That meant garlic bread, the pasta chicken thing and three scoops of chocolate ice cream. Mum says I should try different things but I think you should stick to what you know you like.

'We shouldn't really be having Italian tonight,' said Mum. 'I bought a lasagne for tomorrow as Dad and I are going out.'

'I'm out too,' I said. 'With the Tribers.'

'More for us, Flo,' said Amy.

'Can we have it in front of the telly?'

Two answers came at once, 'No,' from Mum, 'Yes,' from Amy.

Followed by, 'OK, but on a tray,' from Mum.

No one asked me where I was going, which was good as I didn't know. If I had known, I wouldn't have been going.

Out For Tea

'Sorry?' I said. I'd obviously not heard right. Too much swimming isn't good for your hearing.

'Callum's,' Jonno said again.

What sounds like Callum's? I thought. *Kelly's. Connor's. Colin's.*

'I know,' said Fifty in a doom-filled voice. 'I couldn't believe it either.'

What couldn't he believe? That we were going to Kelly's or Connor's or Colin's?

'Wait till Copper Pie gets here. He'll have a fit,' said Bee.

Why will he have a fit? Because he doesn't like Kelly or Connor or Colin or whoever's house it is we're going to, I thought.

'Don't blame me,' said Jonno. 'Callum's mum didn't give me a chance to think of an excuse. Before I had a hope of coming up with a reason why I couldn't come for tea, she was arranging the time.'

I hadn't misheard. It wasn't Kelly's or Connor's or Colin's, we were going to Callum's for tea. The information trickled very slowly into my brain, like water finding a way through clay.

'It's so embarrassing,' said Bee. 'We'll have to pretend we're friends. What will we talk about?'

'School?' said Fifty.

'Good idea,' said Bee. 'Let's talk about all the good times we've had with Callum. That shouldn't take long.' She was really miffed. I was hoping she'd refuse to go. I could do the same. Copper Pie probably would anyway. Jonno and Fifty could go on their own.

Even though I tried to believe that might happen, I knew it wouldn't. It's not Tribish to dump on your mates. It's not Tribish to split up – Tribers stay together. It's also not Tribish to go to tea with your enemy, but that seemed to be what was happening. Although I still wasn't sure why.

'Why are we going to Callum's?'

Jonno sighed, did the pushing-back-his-springy-hair thing and then answered. 'Callum's mum reckons it was because of what we said when we went round that Callum blurted out the truth. She thinks we're friends and that we helped him. So the tea's a reward, kind of.'

Funny sort of reward, I thought.

'Funny sort of reward,' said Fifty.

Get out of my head, I thought.

'Let's not tell Copper Pie till we get there,' said Bee. That definitely wasn't Tribish. 'Or he won't come.'

'Where won't I come?' said Copper Pie. He didn't step into the Tribehouse. He stood in the doorway.

We all looked at Jonno (except Jonno, who looked back at us).

'You're the one with the magic words,' said Fifty. 'Go on.'

He persuaded C.P. last time. All he needed to do was the same again. But Jonno didn't say anything, for longer than a few seconds. Then he said, 'OK. How about we give you a box of beef crisps.' He paused. *'And* we stand in goal for you every lunchtime for a week so you can take shots at us, at the goal, I mean?'

Copper Pie narrowed his eyes. 'Why?'

Jonno screwed up his face, as though he was trying to keep the words in, but they shot out. 'We're all going to Callum's for tea.'

'All,' said Bee.

'Same,' said Fifty.

I was waiting for Copper Pie to reverse straight back out, but he didn't.

'A box of beef crisps, goalies all week, and Keener does my homework, and I'm not saying anything at Hog's house. Not a word.'

'Done,' said Jonno. He put out his hand. Four others followed. The Tribe handshake sealed the deal.

Thali
Time

Callum's mum answered the door. She was wearing shorts and a T-shirt and looked more like a friend of Amy's than a mum, and completely different from last time we saw her.

'We're eating in about ten minutes. Go through to the back. Callum's out there.'

Jonno was in front. He said 'Thanks,' and headed in the direction she'd pointed towards. Callum was sitting on the grass, holding a brown rabbit.

Bee instantly forgot he was the enemy. 'That's so sweet,' she gushed. 'What's it called?'

'Dizzy,' said Callum. 'It's a girl.'

'Can I hold her?'

'Sure. She'll go to anyone. Unlike Pinkerton.'

'Who's Pinkerton?' said Jonno.

'The anti-social rabbit,' said Callum. 'He's around some-where.'

What did he mean? *He's around somewhere. Aren't rabbits meant to be in a cage?*

Callum's mum came out of the kitchen door holding a black rabbit. 'Keep him out here, Callum. He's under my feet.' She put him down on the ground, near me. Pinkerton seemed to be looking at my trainer.

'Stroke him, Keener,' said Bee.

No way, I thought. Rabbits have teeth.

Fifty crouched down and let Pinkerton sniff his fingers. 'Hello, Pinkerton.'

What is it about animals that makes people go soppy?

'I wish I could have a pet,' said Jonno.

'I wish we could have less,' said Callum.

'Why? What else have you got?' said Jonno.

'We've got two cats, two rabbits and a corn snake.'

'Can I see the snake?' said Jonno.

'Sure.' Callum and Jonno disappeared inside. We stayed with the rabbits. So far so good. All we had to do was scoff our tea and The Strange Case of the Pink-smeared Board and the Suspended Boy would be over.

'Supper, everyone,' shouted Callum's mum. We didn't know what to do with the rabbits so Bee gave Dizzy to me and went to ask. The rabbit was warm and quite nice to hold.

'She said bring them in. They're house rabbits.' Bee

made a what's-a-house-rabbit? face with matching what's-a-house-rabbit? hands.

I carried Dizzy and Fifty carried Pinkerton. We went through the kitchen and into a kind of sunroom – all glass and open windows. On the table there were loads of little metal dishes with totally unrecognisable food.

'I hope you all like Indian food,' said Callum's mum.

'Absolutely,' said Bee. She sat down. Copper Pie did too. (He was doing what he said he would – saying nothing – but he looked quite interested in eating.) Jonno and Callum came in and sat next to each other. Fifty and I stood like lemons holding the bunnies (not that lemons generally hold bunnies).

'Pop them down,' said Callum's mum. *Down where?* I looked at Fifty for a clue. He was clueless.

'On the carpet,' said Callum.

'Right.' We dumped Pinkerton and Dizzy, but I kept a roving eye on them. I didn't want to do a Miss Walsh and kick one.

Fifty sat between Bee and Jonno. I got Callum and his mum. Great!

'OK,' she said. 'This is a thali. My favourite meal because none of it's cooked by me – all I had to do was pick it up – and because I love meals with loads of bits.' She smiled. 'Rice, vegetable curry, chapatis, yoghurt, chicken something or other, chutneys and dhal. Oh and paneer, that's Indian cheese. Tuck in.'

Copper Pie didn't need telling twice. Nor did Jonno. I hung back waiting to see what went with what in case there was an order. The answer was it all went together. And it was all right, apart from the red chutney which was spicy hot.

Callum's mum had some red wine. We had Coke.

All through the meal there was chatting. Not uncomfortable, this-is-so-awkward chatting, easy quite funny as-though-we-were-at-Bee's-house chatting. Weird. Don't get the wrong idea – I wasn't about to suggest Callum join Tribe (not that anyone can) but it was a breeze compared to how I thought it would be. I wondered where Callum's dad was.

'So, Keener.' Callum's mum turned to me. I hadn't said a word at dinner. 'How long have you been friends with Callum?'

The instant raspberry face was accompanied by sweaty armpits. *Think of something, Keener.* I opened my mouth to encourage something to come out – it sometimes works. But not this time.

'We've all been in the same class for ages,' said Fifty.

Thank you.

The dishes were all cleared by Callum and Bee. Pudding came next. I was on high alert in case she tried to make me talk again but I think she thought I was shy, or stupid, or both and she didn't ask anything else. Fine by me.

'We'd better be going,' said Fifty when our bowls were

184

clean. 'Thank you for the thali. It was really nice.' He smiled his cutest I've-got-curly-black-hair-and-rosy-cheeks smile.

'So soon?' she said.

I didn't want to risk having to stay so I finally spoke. 'Yes. We've got to go.'

'Well, it's been lovely to have company. It's quiet with just the two of us.' *Maybe Callum doesn't have a dad*, I thought. 'Come any time,' she said. She put her arm round Callum . . . and kissed him! That was worth storing up if we needed ammunition when we went back to the usual warring between Tribe and Callum. After all, having a nice mum and nice rabbits didn't mean *he* was nice.

Everyone said 'Bye.' Excellent. Dinner was done.

Except on the way home Bee had a proposal.

'I know we said no one can leave and no one can join, but we made the rule so we can change it.' I knew what she was going to say. No way!

I stared straight at Bee. 'But it's in the manifesto you wrote . . . the one that's in the Tribehouse.' (Bee insisted on writing down our aims and stuff in a posh way on posh paper – it's rolled up at the back of the safe.)

'Exactly, Keener. I wrote it. I can change it.'

I could tell the others were all nudging each other behind me, and whispering. It wasn't surprising – I don't usually pick a fight with Bee, for obvious reasons. But someone needed to do something before she decided to crown Callum as Chief Triber. As I turned round to make sure they were supporting me I saw Jonno wink at Bee. *Surely he didn't agree with her.* I searched the faces of my fellow Tribers. *Say something!* No one looked me in the eye. They all seemed a bit uncomfortable.

'The black rabbit was cute, wasn't it?' said Fifty. *Not Fifty too!* This was a mutiny.

'And his snake was amazing. He feeds it baby mice,' said Jonno. 'You buy them frozen, like scallops.'

It was unbelievable. They were on Bee's side. The Strange Case of the Pink-smeared Board and the Suspended Boy was in danger of turning out very badly indeed. I couldn't understand why Copper Pie wasn't shouting 'No way can Callum be a Triber.' He was bound to be on my side. I nudged him.

'What?' he said.

I stuttered something. I was so het up I couldn't get the words out. (Actually I didn't know what the words were.) *How could the Tribers be so stupid? So we had a nice tea, that didn't change anything. So he had pets, who cares? Callum was still Callum. Full stop.* I shook my head, desperate to find a way of stopping the madness.

Copper Pie started laughing at me. Not very nice, but that's what he's like sometimes.

I tried again. 'But —'

Bee doubled over and started groaning. Jonno's face collapsed with giggles. Fifty was obviously trying not to laugh. *Oh great!* My stupid Triber mates, who wanted to make friends with Hog all because of a rabbit and a snake, were in fits because I'd stumbled over a couple of words. I thought about walking off.

Bee put her hand on my shoulder, and snorted in my ear like a pig.

'Go away,' I said.

'Keener.' She didn't say anything except my name because she was too busy being in stitches. 'It's a joke.'

I didn't see what it was about me that was a joke. Even Fifty, who I spend most time with, was laughing now.

'It's a joke, Keener,' he said. More loud laughing. That was it. I'd had enough. I walked off, fast. My face was hot and I was really angry.

Jonno caught up with me. 'Stop, Keener. Stop a minute.'

I stopped. 'Finished laughing at me?' I said.

'Sorry, Keener. It was a joke about Callum, not you. We don't want him to be a Triber. It was a joke, that's all. Bee didn't mean that thing about changing our rule that no one can join, but you sounded so . . . outraged, like someone complaining on the radio. And then when you turned round she winked at us and we all got the idea and . . . pretended to agree. It was a wind up, that's all. Sorry.'

The others all caught up. They had serious faces. I thought about saying *Ha ha that's funny, my name's Bugs Bunny*, but that's what Flo says and it sounds really silly (which is exactly how I felt), so I didn't say anything.

'Sorry,' said Bee.

'Sorry,' said Copper Pie.

'Same,' said Fifty.

Even though I was still cross, I couldn't help feeling relieved. It was finally over. It would have been nicer if they hadn't decided to follow thali time with tease-Keener time but I could see it was mildly funny that I fell for it.

'I'll let you off,' I said.

'You are a bit of a twit, believing we'd change our minds that easily,' said Bee.

'It's weird though, that Callum's such a pain at school when his mum's so nice,' said Fifty.

'I don't think it's weird,' said Jonno. 'It's stupid to think that all mean people have mean parents and all nice people have nice parents and all kids who lie have parents who lie.'

'Too right,' said Copper Pie. 'I'm lovely and my mum's terrible.' This time it was me who laughed my head off.

'And my mum's a nutter and I'm completely sane,' said Fifty, making a completely insane face.

'And my mum's a doctor,' I said, 'and I can't stand blood.'

Bee was right – as usual. I was a twit. I should have had more faith. Tribe had been tested loads of times, and every time we'd come out on top. I slapped my hand down and we did a Tribe handshake with whooping noises.

After all, it takes more than a snake, two rabbits, two cats and a thali to make a Triber.

TRIBE Five friends have
fun and adventures

T M Alexander

Monkey
Bars
and
Rubber
Ducks

Why is Copper Pie bunking off school at
lunchtime? When the other Tribers find out,
they can't help getting involved and they're
soon in trouble (again).

Then it's the school camping trip, where
Team Tribe build rafts, tell jokes, race rubber ducks
and finally face the scary assault course.
Will Fifty manage to conquer his fear?

It's non-stop for Tribe.

Coming Soon

T. M. Alexander's favourite colour is green. When she's not writing, she's either cycling around on her bright green bike or swimming in the green water of her local lake. She doesn't have a pet, but if she did, it would be green.

Get to know the Tribers!

www.tribers.co.uk

Have you read these other Tribe books?

Jonno Joins
Goodbye, Copper Pie